Two bad fairies attended the christening and, hey presto, it was a case of 'Which pig is the princess?' The poor king was in despair, for his bewitched little daughter the princess-pig was absolutely indistinguishable from her common little piggy friend, no matter what tests were applied. When it came to peas under the mattress both little pigs rummaged out the peas and ate them, and when dishes of pearls and potato peelings were placed before them they both dived unhesitatingly for the potato peelings. So how *did* they find out the true princess? Read and discover.

But this is only one of the brilliantly varied stories in this magical, haunting, myriad-mooded volume. There's the sad, spell-binding tale of Johnny Rigby; about tears locked in a heart and a heart locked in a river; the story of a confiding little ghost puppy; and a weird history of a baby whose cradle lay across the wolf's path, and what befell him. Harriet and Mark Armitage, the children with the pet unicorn, are here again engaged upon an adventure concerning a griffin's egg; and of course there is the fairy tale of the title about a little orphan girl called Nerryn and the magic harp of fishbones she made in memory of her lost father.

Joan Aiken's books are a perpetual and delightful surprise. She must be the most versatile children's writer living, with her bounding, boundless optimism, her sense of tragedy and pathos, her intuition, her romance, her mystery, her humour, her appreciation of humanity and her sometimes devastating criticism. She has four other books of stories in Puffins, *A Necklace of Raindrops*, *A Small Pinch of Weather*, *The Kingdom Under the Sea* and *All But a Few*, and also five novels, *The Wolves of Willoughby Chase*, *Black Hearts in Battersea*, *Night Birds on Nantucket*, *The Whispering Mountain* and *The Cuckoo Tree*.

For readers of ten and over.

JOAN AIKEN

A Harp of Fishbones
and Other Stories

ILLUSTRATED BY PAT MARRIOTT

PUFFIN BOOKS

Puffin Books, Penguin Books Ltd, Harmondsworth, Middlesex, England
Penguin Books Australia Ltd, Ringwood, Victoria, Australia
Penguin Books Canada Ltd, 41 Steelcase Road West, Markham, Ontario, Canada
Penguin Books (N.Z.) Ltd, 182-190 Wairau Road, Auckland 10, New Zealand

—

This collection first published by Jonathan Cape 1972
Published in Puffin Books 1975

—

Copyright © Joan Aiken 1960, 1967, 1969, 1970, 1971, 1972
Illustrations copyright © by Jonathan Cape Ltd, 1972

—

Made and printed in Great Britain
by Richard Clay (The Chaucer Press), Ltd.,
Bungay, Suffolk
Set in Monotype Garamond

FOR MAX

Contents

The author and publishers are grateful to the editors and publishers of the following books and magazines for permission to reprint: *Miscellany 4*, Oxford University Press ('A Harp of Fishbones'), *Magpie Book of Stories*, Purnell/Bancroft ('The Boy with a Wolf's Foot'), *Allsorts 4*, Macmillan ('The Lost Five Minutes'), *The World of Ballet*, Collins ('The Rose of Puddle Fratrum'), *Puffin Post* ('A Jar of Cobblestones' and 'Humblepuppy'), *Young Winter's Tales 2*, Macmillan ('A Long Day Without Water'), *Argosy* ('The River Boy'), *Allsorts 3*, Macmillan ('The Gift Pig') and *The Friday Miracle and Other Stories*, Puffin Books ('The Dark Streets of Kimball's Green').

A Harp of Fishbones

LITTLE Nerryn lived in the half-ruined mill at the upper end of the village, where the stream ran out of the forest. The old miller's name was Timorash, but she called him uncle. Her own father and mother were dead, long before she could remember. Timorash was no real kin, nor was he particularly kind to her; he was a lazy old man. He never troubled to grow corn as the other people in the village did, little patches in the clearing below the village before the forest began again. When people brought him corn to grind he took one-fifth of it as his fee and this, with wild plums which Nerryn gathered and dried, and carp from the deep millpool, kept him and the child fed through the short bright summers and the long silent winters.

Nerryn learned to do the cooking when she was seven or eight; she toasted fish on sticks over the fire and baked cakes of bread on a flat stone; Timorash beat her if the food was burnt, but it mostly was, just the same, because so often half her mind would be elsewhere, listening to the bell-like call of a bird or pondering about what made the difference between the stream's voice in winter and in summer. When she was a little older Timorash taught her how to work the mill, opening the sluice-gate so that the green, clear mountain water could hurl down against the great wooden paddle-wheel. Nerryn liked this much better, since she already spent hours watching the stream endlessly pouring and plaiting down its narrow passage. Old Timorash had hoped that now he would be able to give up work altogether and lie in the sun all day, or

crouch by the fire, slowly adding one stick after another
and dreaming about barley wine. But Nerryn forgot to
take flour in payment from the villagers, who were in no
hurry to remind her, so the old man angrily decided that
this plan would not answer, and sent her out to work.

First she worked for one household, then for another.

The people of the village had come from the plains;
they were surly, big-boned, and lank, with tow-coloured
hair and pale eyes; even the children seldom spoke. Little
Nerryn sometimes wondered, looking at her reflection in
the millpool, how it was that she should be so different
from them, small and brown-skinned, with dark hair like
a bird's feathers and hazelnut eyes. But it was no use
asking questions of old Timorash, who never answered
except by grunting or throwing a clod of earth at her.
Another difference was that she loved to chatter, and this
was perhaps the main reason why the people she worked
for soon sent her packing.

There were other reasons too, for, though Nerryn was
willing enough to work, things often distracted her.

'She let the bread burn while she ran outside to listen
to a curlew,' said one.

'When she was helping me cut the hay she asked so
many questions that my ears have ached for three days,'
complained another.

'Instead of scaring off the birds from my corn-patch she
sat with her chin on her fists, watching them gobble down
half a winter's supply and whistling to them!' grumbled a
third.

Nobody would keep her more than a few days, and she
had plenty of beatings, especially from Timorash, who
had hoped that her earnings would pay for a keg of
barley wine. Once in his life he had had a whole keg, and
he still felt angry when he remembered that it was finished.

At last Nerryn went to work for an old woman who

lived in a tumbledown hut at the bottom of the street. Her name was Saroon and she was by far the oldest in the village, so withered and wrinkled that most people thought she was a witch; besides, she knew when it was going to rain and was the only person in the place who did not fear to venture a little way into the forest. But she was growing weak now, and stiff, and wanted somebody to help dig her corn-patch and cut wood. Nevertheless she hardly seemed to welcome help when it came. As Nerryn moved about at the tasks she was set, the old woman's little red-rimmed eyes followed her suspiciously; she hobbled round the hut watching through cracks, grumbling and chuntering to herself, never losing sight of the girl for a moment, like some cross-grained old animal that sees a stranger near its burrow.

On the fourth day she said,

'You're singing, girl.'

'I – I'm sorry,' Nerryn stammered. 'I didn't mean to – I wasn't thinking. Don't beat me, please.'

'Humph,' said the old woman, but she did not beat Nerryn that time. And next day, watching through the window-hole while Nerryn chopped wood, she said,

'You're not singing.'

Nerryn jumped. She had not known the old woman was so near.

'I thought you didn't like me to,' she faltered.

'I didn't say so, did I?'

Muttering, the old woman stumped off to the back of the hut and began to sort through a box of mildewy nuts. 'As if I should care,' Nerryn heard her grumble, 'whether the girl sings or not!' But next day she put her head out of the door, while Nerryn hoed the corn-patch, and said,

'Sing, child!'

Nerryn looked at her, doubtful and timid, to see if she really meant it, but she nodded her head energetically, till the tangled grey locks jounced on her shoulders, and repeated,

'Sing!'

So presently the clear, tiny thread of Nerryn's song began again as she sliced off the weeds; and old Saroon came out and sat on an upturned log beside the door, pounding roots for soup and mumbling to herself in time to the sound. And at the end of the week she did not dismiss the girl, as everyone else had done, though what she paid was so little that Timorash grumbled every time Nerryn brought it home. At this rate twenty years would go by before he had saved enough for a keg of barley wine.

One day Saroon said,

'Your father used to sing.'

This was the first time anyone had spoken of him.

'Oh,' Nerryn cried, forgetting her fear of the old woman. 'Tell me about him.'

'Why should I?' old Saroon said sourly. 'He never did anything for *me*.' And she hobbled off to fetch a pot of water. But later she relented and said,

'His hair was the colour of ash buds, like yours. And he carried a harp.'

'A harp, what is a harp?'

'Oh, don't pester, child. I'm busy.'

But another day she said, 'A harp is a thing to make music. His was a gold one, but it was broken.'

'Gold, what is gold?'

'This,' said the old woman, and she pulled out a small, thin disc which she wore on a cord of plaited grass round her neck.

'Why!' Nerryn exclaimed. 'Everybody in the village has one of those except Timorash and me. I've often asked what they were but no one would answer.'

'They are gold. When your father went off and left you and the harp with Timorash, the old man ground up the harp between the millstones. And he melted down the gold powder and made it into these little circles and sold them to everybody in the village, and bought a keg of barley wine. He told us they would bring good luck. But I have never had any good luck and that was a long time ago. And Timorash has long since drunk all his barley wine.'

'Where did my father go?' asked Nerryn.

'Into the forest,' the old woman snapped. 'I could have told him he was in for trouble. I could have warned him. But he never asked *my* advice.'

She sniffed, and set a pot of herbs boiling on the fire. And Nerryn could get no more out of her that day.

But little by little, as time passed, more came out.

'Your father came from over the mountains. High up yonder, he said, there was a great city, with houses and palaces and temples, and as many rich people as there are fish in the millpool. Best of all, there was always music playing in the streets and houses and in the temples. But then the goddess of the mountain became angry, and fire burst out of a crack in the hillside. And then a great cold came, so that people froze where they stood. Your father said he only just managed to escape with you by running very fast. Your mother had died in the fire.'

'Where was he going?'

'The king of the city had ordered him to go for help.'

'What sort of help?'

'Don't ask *me*,' the old woman grumbled. 'You'd think he'd have settled down here like a person of sense, and mended his harp. But no, on he must go, leaving you behind so that he could travel faster. He said he'd fetch you again on his way back. But of course he never did come back – one day I found his bones in the forest. The birds must have killed him.'

'How do you *know* they were my father's bones?'

'Because of the tablet he carried. See, here it is, with his name on it, Heramon the harper.'

'Tell me more about the harp!'

'It was shaped like this,' the old woman said. They were washing clothes by the stream, and she drew with her finger in the mud. 'Like this, and it had golden strings across, so. All but one of the strings had melted in the fire from the mountain. Even on just one string he could make very beautiful music, that would force you to stop whatever you were doing and listen. It is a pity he had to leave the harp behind. Timorash wanted it as payment for looking after you. If your father had taken the harp with him, perhaps he would have been able to reach the other side of the forest.'

Nerryn thought about this story a great deal. For the next few weeks she did even less work than usual and was mostly to be found squatting with her chin on her fists by the side of the stream. Saroon beat her, but not very hard. Then one day Nerryn said,

'I shall make a harp.'

'Hah!' sniffed the old woman. 'You! What do you know of such things?'

After a few minutes she asked,

'What will you make it from?'

Nerryn said, 'I shall make it of fishbones. Some of the biggest carp in the millpool have bones as thick as my wrist, and they are very strong.'

'Timorash will never allow it.'

'I shall wait till he is asleep, then.'

So Nerryn waited till night, and then she took a chunk of rotten wood, which glows in the dark, and dived into the deep millpool, swimming down and down to the depths where the biggest carp lurk, among the mud and weeds and old sunken logs.

When they saw the glimmer of the wood through the

water, all the fish came nosing and nibbling and swimming round Nerryn, curious to find if this thing which shone so strangely was good to eat. She waited as long as she could bear it, holding her breath, till a great barrel-shaped monster slid nudging right up against her; then, quick as a flash, she wrapped her arms round his slippery sides and fled up with a bursting heart to the surface.

Much to her surprise, old Saroon was there, waiting in the dark on the bank. But the old woman only said,

'You had better bring the carp to my hut. After all, you want no more than the bones, and it would be a pity to waste all that good meat. I can live on it for a week.' So she cut the meat off the bones, which were coal-black but had a sheen on them like mother-of-pearl. Nerryn dried them by the fire, and then she joined together the three biggest, notching them to fit, and cementing them with a glue she made by boiling some of the smaller bones together. She used long, thin, strong bones for strings, joining them to the frame in the same manner.

All the time old Saroon watched closely. Sometimes she would say,

'That was not the way of it. Heramon's harp was wider,' or 'You are putting the strings too far apart. There should be more of them, and they should be tighter.'

When at last it was done, she said,

'Now you must hang it in the sun to dry.'

So for three days the harp hung drying in the sun and wind. At night Saroon took it into her hut and covered it with a cloth. On the fourth day she said,

'Now, play!'

Nerryn rubbed her finger across the strings, and they gave out a liquid murmur, like that of a stream running over pebbles, under a bridge. She plucked a string, and the noise was like that a drop of water makes, falling in a hollow place.

'That will be music,' old Saroon said, nodding her head, satisfied. 'It is not quite the same as the sound from your father's harp, but it is music. Now you shall play me tunes every day, and I shall sit in the sun and listen.'

'No,' said Nerryn, 'for if Timorash hears me playing he will take the harp away and break it or sell it. I shall go to my father's city and see if I can find any of his kin there.'

At this old Saroon was very angry. 'Here have I taken all these pains to help you, and what reward do I get for it? How much pleasure do you think I have, living among dolts in this dismal place? I was not born here, any more than you were. You could at least play to me at night, when Timorash is asleep.'

'Well, I will play to you for seven nights,' Nerryn said.

Each night old Saroon tried to persuade her not to go, and she tried harder as Nerryn became more skilful in playing, and drew from the fishbone harp a curious watery music, like the songs that birds sing when it is raining. But Nerryn would not be persuaded to stay, and when she saw this, on the seventh night, Saroon said,

'I suppose I shall have to tell you how to go through the forest. Otherwise you will certainly die, as your father did. When you go among the trees you will find that the grass underfoot is thick and strong and hairy, and the farther you go, the higher it grows, as high as your waist. And it is sticky and clings to you, so that you can only go forward slowly, one step at a time. Then, in the middle of the forest, perched in the branches, are vultures who will drop on you and peck you to death if you stand still for more than a minute.'

'How do you know all this?' Nerryn said.

'I have tried many times to go through the forest, but it is too far for me; I grow tired and have to turn back. The vultures take no notice of me, I am too old and withered, but a tender young piece like you would be just what they fancy.'

'Then what must I do?' Nerryn asked.

'You must play music on your harp till they fall asleep; then, while they sleep, cut the grass with your knife and go forward as fast as you can.'

Nerryn said, 'If I cut you enough fuel for a month, and catch you another carp, and gather you a bushel of nuts, will you give me your little gold circle, or my father's tablet?'

But this Saroon would not do. She did, though, break off the corner of the tablet which had Heramon the harper's name on it, and give that to Nerryn.

'But don't blame me,' she said sourly, 'if you find the city all burnt and frozen, with not a living soul to walk its streets.'

'Oh, it will all have been rebuilt by this time,' Nerryn said. 'I shall find my father's people, or my mother's, and I shall come back for you, riding a white mule and leading another.'

'Fairy tales!' old Saroon said angrily. 'Be off with you, then. If you don't wish to stay I'm sure I don't want you idling about the place. All the work you've done this last week I could have done better myself in half an hour. Drat the woodsmoke! It gets in a body's eyes till they can't see a thing.' And she hobbled into the hut, working her mouth sourly and rubbing her eyes with the back of her hand.

Nerryn ran into the forest, going cornerways up the mountain, so as not to pass too close to the mill where old Timorash lay sleeping in the sun.

Soon she had to slow down because the way was so steep. And the grass grew thicker and thicker, hairy, sticky, all twined and matted together, as high as her waist. Presently, as she hacked and cut at it with her bone knife, she heard a harsh croaking and flapping above her. She looked up, and saw two grey vultures perched on a branch, leaning forward to peer down at her. Their wings were twice the length of a man's arm and they had long, wrinkled, black, leathery necks and little fierce yellow eyes. As she stood, two more, then five, ten, twenty others came rousting through the branches, and all perched round about, craning down their long black necks, swaying back and forth, keeping balanced by the way they opened and shut their wings.

Nerryn felt very much afraid of them, but she unslung the harp from her back and began to play a soft, trickling tune, like rain falling on a deep pool. Very soon the vultures sank their necks down between their shoulders and closed their eyes. They sat perfectly still.

When she was certain they were asleep, Nerryn made haste to cut and slash at the grass. She was several hundred yards on her way before the vultures woke and came cawing and jostling through the branches to cluster again just overhead. Quickly she pulled the harp round and strummed on its fishbone strings until once again, lulled by the music, the vultures sank their heads between their grey wings and slept. Then she went back to cutting the grass, as fast as she could.

It was a long, tiring way. Soon she grew so weary that she could hardly push one foot ahead of the other, and it was hard to keep awake; once she only just roused in time when a vulture, swooping down, missed her with his beak and instead struck the harp on her back with a loud strange twang that set echoes scampering through the trees.

At last the forest began to thin and dwindle; here the tree-trunks and branches were all draped about with grey-green moss, like long dangling hanks of sheepswool. Moss grew on the rocky ground, too, in a thick carpet. When she reached this part, Nerryn could go on safely;

the vultures rose in an angry flock and flew back with harsh croaks of disappointment, for they feared the trailing moss would wind round their wings and trap them.

As soon as she reached the edge of the trees Nerryn lay down in a deep tussock of moss and fell fast asleep.

She was so tired that she slept almost till nightfall, but then the cold woke her. It was bitter on the bare mountain-side; the ground was all crisp with white frost, and when Nerryn started walking uphill she crunched through it, leaving deep black footprints. Unless she kept moving she knew that she would probably die of cold, so she climbed on, higher and higher; the stars came out, showing more frost-covered slopes ahead and all around, while the forest far below curled round the flank of the mountain like black fur.

Through the night she went on climbing and by sunrise she had reached the foot of a steep slope of ice-covered boulders. When she tried to climb over these she only slipped back again.

What shall I do now? Nerryn wondered. She stood blowing on her frozen fingers and thought, 'I must go on or I shall die here of cold. I will play a tune on the harp to warm my fingers and my wits.'

She unslung the harp. It was hard to play, for her fingers were almost numb and at first refused to obey but, while she had climbed the hill, a very sweet, lively tune had come into her head, and she struggled and struggled until her stubborn fingers found the right notes to play it. Once she played the tune – twice – and the stones on the slope above began to roll and shift. She played a third time and, with a thunderous roar, the whole pile broke loose and went sliding down the mountain-side. Nerryn was only just able to dart aside out of the way before the frozen mass careered past, sending up a smoking dust of ice.

Trembling a little, she went on up the hill, and now she came to a gate in a great wall, set about with towers. The gate stood open, and so she walked through.

'Surely this must be my father's city,' she thought.

But when she stood inside the gate, her heart sank, and she remembered old Saroon's words. For the city that must once have been bright with gold and coloured stone and gay with music was all silent; not a soul walked the streets and the houses, under their thick covering of frost, were burnt and blackened by fire.

And, what was still more frightening, when Nerryn looked through the doorways into the houses, she could see people standing or sitting or lying, frozen still like statues, as the cold had caught them while they worked, or slept, or sat at dinner.

'Where shall I go now?' she thought. 'It would have been better to stay with Saroon in the forest. When night comes I shall only freeze to death in this place.'

But still she went on, almost tiptoeing in the frosty silence of the city, looking into doorways and through gates, until she came to a building that was larger than any other, built with a high roof and many pillars of white marble. The fire had not touched it.

'This must be the temple,' she thought, remembering the tale Saroon had told, and she walked between the pillars, which glittered like white candles in the light from the rising sun. Inside there was a vast hall, and many people standing frozen, just as they had been when they came to pray for deliverance from their trouble. They had offerings with them, honey and cakes and white doves and lambs and precious ointment. At the back of the hall the people wore rough clothes of homespun cloth, but farther forward Nerryn saw wonderful robes, embroidered with gold and copper thread, made of rich materials, trimmed with fur and sparkling stones. And up in the very front, kneeling on the steps of the altar, was a man who was finer than all the rest and Nerryn thought he must have been the king himself. His hair and long beard were white, his cloak was purple, and on his head were three crowns, one gold, one copper, and one of ivory. Nerryn stole up to him and touched the fingers that held a gold staff, but they were ice-cold and still as marble, like all the rest.

A sadness came over her as she looked at the people and she thought, 'What use to them are their fine robes now? Why did the goddess punish them? What did they do wrong?'

But there was no answer to her question.

'I had better leave this place before I am frozen as well,' she thought. 'The goddess may be angry with me too, for coming here. But first I will play for her on my harp, as I have not brought any offering.'

So she took her harp and began to play. She played all the tunes she could remember, and last of all she played the one that had come into her head as she climbed the mountain.

At the noise of her playing, frost began to fall in white showers from the roof of the temple, and from the rafters and pillars and the clothes of the motionless people. Then the king sneezed. Then there was a stirring noise, like the sound of a winter stream when the ice begins to melt. Then someone laughed – a loud, clear laugh. And, just as, outside the town, the pile of frozen rocks had started to move and topple when Nerryn played, so now the whole gathering of people began to stretch themselves, and turn round, and look at one another, and smile. And as she went on playing they began to dance.

The dancing spread, out of the temple and down the

streets. People in the houses stood up and danced. Still dancing, they fetched brooms and swept away the heaps of frost that kept falling from the rooftops with the sound of the music. They fetched old wooden pipes and tabors out of cellars that had escaped the fire, so that when Nerryn stopped playing at last, quite tired out, the music still went on. All day and all night, for thirty days, the music lasted, until the houses were rebuilt, the streets clean, and not a speck of frost remained in the city.

But the king beckoned Nerryn aside when she stopped playing and they sat down on the steps of the temple.

'My child,' he said, 'where did you get that harp?'

'Sir, I made it out of fishbones after a picture of my father's harp that an old woman made for me.'

'And what was your father's name, child, and where is he now?'

'Sir, he is dead in the forest, but here is a piece of a tablet with his name on it.'

And Nerryn held out the little fragment with Heramon the harper's name written. When he saw it, great tears formed in the king's eyes and began to roll down his cheeks.

'Sir,' Nerryn said, 'what is the matter? Why do you weep?'

'I weep for my son Heramon, who is lost, and I weep for joy because my grandchild has returned to me.'

Then the king embraced Nerryn and took her to his palace and had robes of fur and velvet put on her, and there was great happiness and much feasting. And the king told Nerryn how, many years ago, the goddess was angered because the people had grown so greedy for gold from her mountain that they spent their lives in digging and mining, day and night, and forgot to honour her with music, in her temple and in the streets, as they had been used to do. They made tools of gold, and plates and dishes and musical instruments; everything that could be was made of gold. So at last the goddess appeared among them, terrible with rage, and put a curse on them, of burning and freezing.

'Since you prefer gold, got by burrowing in the earth, to the music that should honour me,' she said, 'you may keep your golden toys and little good may they do you! Let your golden harps and trumpets be silent, your flutes and pipes be dumb! I shall not come among you again until I am summoned by notes from a harp that is not made of gold, nor of silver, nor any precious metal, a harp that has never touched the earth but came from deep water, a harp that no man has ever played.'

Then fire burst out of the mountain, destroying houses and killing many people. The king ordered his son Heramon, who was the bravest man in the city, to cross the dangerous forest and seek far and wide until he should find the harp of which the goddess spoke. Before Heramon could depart a great cold had struck, freezing people where they stood; only just in time he caught up his little daughter from her cradle and carried her away with him.

'But now you are come back,' the old king said, 'you shall be queen after me, and we shall take care that the goddess is honoured with music every day, in the temple and in the streets. And we will order everything that is made of gold to be thrown into the mountain torrent, so that nobody ever again shall be tempted to worship gold before the goddess.'

So this was done, the king himself being the first to throw away his golden crown and staff. The river carried all the golden things down through the forest until they came to rest in Timorash's millpool, and one day, when he was fishing for carp, he pulled out the crown. Overjoyed, he ground it to powder and sold it to his neighbours for barley wine. Then he returned to the pool, hoping for more gold, but by now he was so drunk that he fell in and was drowned among a clutter of golden spades and trumpets and goblets and pickaxes.

But long before this Nerryn, with her harp on her back and astride of a white mule with knives bound to its hoofs, had ridden down the mountain to fetch Saroon as she had promised. She passed the forest safely, playing music for the vultures while the mule cut its way through the long grass. Nobody in the village recognized her, so splendidly was she dressed in fur and scarlet.

But when she came to where Saroon's hut had stood, the ground was bare, nor was there any trace that a dwelling had ever been there. And when she asked for Saroon, nobody knew the name, and the whole village declared that such a person had never been there.

Amazed and sorrowful, Nerryn returned to her grandfather. But one day, not long after, when she was alone, praying in the temple of the goddess, she heard a voice that said,

'Sing, child!'

And Nerryn was greatly astonished, for she felt she had heard the voice before, though she could not think where.

While she looked about her, wondering, the voice said again,

'Sing!'

And then Nerryn understood, and she laughed, and, taking her harp, sang a song about chopping wood, and about digging, and fishing, and the birds of the forest, and how the stream's voice changes in summer and in winter. For now she knew who had helped her to make her harp of fishbones.

The Boy with a Wolf's Foot

ONCE when I was travelling on a train from Waterloo to Guildford I looked out of the window and saw a boy and a great Alsatian dog running through the fields. Just for a few moments they seemed to be able to run faster than the train.

This is that boy's story.

The night of Will Wilder's birth was one of rain and gale; the wind went hunting along the railway embankment between Worplesdon and Woking like something that has been shut in a cave for twenty years.

Have you ever noticed what a lot of place names begin with a W in that part of the world? There's Wandsworth and Wimbledon, Walton and Weybridge and Worcester Park; there's Witley and Wanborough and West Byfleet; then, farther east, Waddon and Wallington, Woodmansterne, Woodside, Westerham, Warlingham, and Woldingham; it's as if ancient Surrey and Kent had been full of the wailing of wild things in the woods.

Maybe it was the wind that caused the train derailment; anyway, whatever the cause, young Doctor Talisman, who, tired out, had fallen asleep in his non-smoking carriage after coming off duty at the Waterloo Hospital, was woken by a violent grinding jerk and at the same moment found himself flung clean through the train window to land, unhurt but somewhat dazed, in a clump of brambles that luckily broke his fall.

He scrambled through the prickles, trying to rub rain and darkness from his eyes, and discovered that he was standing, as it were, in a loop of train. The middle section had been derailed and sagged down the embankment, almost upside down; the two ends were still on the track. People were running and shouting; lights flared; the rain splashed and hissed on hot metal; the wind howled over all.

Pulling himself together the doctor made his way to the nearest group.

'I'm a medical man,' he said. 'Is anybody in need of help?'

People were glad to turn to him; there were plenty of cuts and bruises and he was kept busy till the ambulances managed to make their way to the spot – which took time, for the crash had happened quite a long way from the nearest road, and they had to come bumping over grass and round bushes and past stacks of timber and bricks, through a bit of dark countryside that was half heath, half waste land, with the River Wey running through it.

'Any seriously hurt?' an ambulance attendant asked, finding the young doctor working among the injured.

'One broken leg; several concussions; and there's one man killed outright,' said the doctor sadly. 'What makes it worse is that he had a young baby with him – born today I'd guess. The child's all right – was thrown clear in his carry-cot. Hasn't even woken.'

At that moment the baby did wake and begin to cry – a faint thread of sound in the roaring of the wind.

'He'd best come along with us,' said the ambulance man, 'till we find someone to claim him. Hear the wind – hark to it blow! You'd think there was a pack of wolves chasing along the embankment.'

Police and firemen arrived on the scene; the doctor was given a lift back to his home in Worplesdon. Next day he went along to the hospital where the injured people had been taken, and inquired after the baby.

'It's a sad thing,' the matron said. 'We've found out his

father had just fetched him from the London hospital where he was born; his mother died there yesterday. Now the father's dead too the child has no relations at all; seems to be alone in the world. They'd just come from Canada, but had no family there. So the baby will have to go to the orphanage. And there's another queer thing: one of his feet is an odd shape, and has fur growing on it; as if the poor child hadn't enough bad luck already.'

Young Doctor Talisman sighed, looking at the dark-haired baby sleeping so peacefully in his hospital cot, still unaware of the troubles he had inherited.

'I'll call in at the orphanage from time to time and see how he goes on,' he promised. 'What's his name?'

'Wilder. Will Wilder. Luckily we found his birth certificate in the father's suitcase. What are you looking for, doctor?'

'I was just wondering what I had done with my watch,' Dr Talisman said. 'But I remember now; I took it off when I was helping to pull hurt people out of the wreckage last night and buckled it on to the branch of a tree growing on the embankment; I'll go back and find it sometime.'

True to his word, the doctor called at Worplesdon Orphanage to see young Will Wilder and, having formed the habit, he went on doing it year after year; became a kind of adopted uncle and, as there was nobody else to do it, took Will for trips to the zoo and the pantomime, days at the beach, and weekends canoeing on the river. No real relatives ever turned up to claim the boy. Nor did the doctor ever marry and have children of his own; somehow he was always too busy looking after his patients to have time for courtship; so a closeness grew between the two of them as year followed year.

Young Will never made friends at school. He was a silent, inturned boy, and kept himself to himself. For one thing his odd foot made him lame, so he could not run fast; he was no good at football or sports, which helped separate him from the others. But though he could not run he loved speed, and went for long rides on a bicycle the doctor gave him; also he loved books and would sit reading for hours on end while everyone else was running and fighting in the playground. And, from being a silent, solitary boy he became a thoughtful, solitary young man. He did well at his exams, but seemed to find it hard to decide on a career. While he was thinking, he took a job in the public library, and lived on his own in a bedsitter. But he still called in on the doctor once or twice a week.

One time when he called in he said, 'I've been reading up the old history of this neighbourhood. And I found that way back, centuries back, there was a whole tribe of Wilders living in these parts.'

'Is that so?' said the doctor with interest. 'Maybe they were your ancestors. Maybe that was why your parents were travelling here, from Canada, to find the place their forefathers had come from. What did they do, those Wilders? Where did they live?'

'They were gypsies and tinkers and charcoal burners,' Will said. 'They lived in tents and carts on a piece of land known as Worplesdon Wilderness. I haven't been able to discover exactly where it was. It seems the Wilders had lived there so long – since Saxon times or before – that they had a sort of squatters' right to the land, although they never built houses on it.'

'You ought to try and find an ancient map of the neighbourhood,' the doctor said, 'and discover where it could have been.' He glanced at his watch – not the watch he had buckled on a tree on the railway embankment, for somehow he had never found time to go back and reclaim that one, but another, given him by a grateful patient. Patients were always giving him presents, because he was a good doctor, and kind as well. 'Dear me, how late it's getting. I must be off to the hospital; I promised to look in on old Mrs Jones.'

They walked to the gate together, Will limping; then Will mounted the bike and pedalled swiftly away. 'I wish something could be done about that foot of his,' the doctor thought, sighing over the contrast between Will's slow, limping walk and his speedy skilful progress on the bike. During the years since Will's babyhood the doctor had read up all the cases of foot troubles he could find, from fallen arches to ingrowing toenails, but he had never come across any case exactly like Will's. 'But there's that new bone specialist just come to the Wimbledon hospital; I'll ask his opinion about it.'

'I've found out a bit more about those Wilders,' Will said, next time he called on the doctor. 'They had a kind of a spooky reputation in the villages round about.'

'Gypsies and people living rough often did in the old days,' said the doctor. 'What were they supposed to do?'

'Anything from stealing chickens to hobnobbing with the devil! People were scared to go past Worplesdon Wilderness at night.'

'I wish we knew where it had been exactly,' said the doctor. 'Maybe where the football fields are now. Oh, by the way, there's a new consultant, Dr Moberley, at the Wimbledon hospital, who'd very much like to have a look at your foot, if you'd agree to go along there some time.'

Will's face closed up, as it always did when his foot was mentioned.

'What's the good?' he said. 'No one can do anything about it. Oh, very well –' as the doctor began to protest. 'To please you I'll go. But it won't be any use.'

'That certainly is a most unusual case,' the consultant said to Dr Talisman when they met at the hospital the following week. 'The only thing at all similar that I've ever come across was a case in India, years ago.'

'Could you do anything for him?'

'I'm not sure. I'll have to consider, and read up some old histories. I'll talk to you again about him.'

But in the meantime Will came to the doctor one evening and said,

'I've decided to go to Canada.'

'Why go there?' Dr Talisman was astonished. For, privately, he thought that in such an outdoor kind of place the boy with his lame foot would be at even more of a disadvantage. But Will surprised him still further by saying,

'The museum has given me a small grant to do some research into legends about wolves.'

'Wolves? I didn't know you were interested in wolves.'

'Oh yes, I am,' said Will. 'I've been interested in wolves for a long time. Ever since I was a child and you used to take me to the zoo, remember?'

Dr Talisman did remember then that Will always stopped for a long time by the wolves' enclosure and seemed as if he would rather stay watching them than look at anything else in the zoo; as if he felt he could learn something important from them.

'You won't be going to Canada for good?' he said. 'I shall miss you, Will.'

'Oh no, I'll be back. I just want to go to a place where there are still wolves wild in the woods. And while I'm over there I'll see if I can find out anything about my parents. Do you remember, among my father's things there was a little book with a couple of addresses in a town called Wilderness, Manitoba? A Mrs Smith and a man called Barney Davies. Of course they may be dead by now but I shall go there and see.'

'When are you off?'

'Tomorrow.'

'But what about Dr Moberley? He was going to think about your case.'

'He wouldn't have been able to do anything,' said Will, and limped down the garden to where his bike leaned against the fence.

'What about the Worplesdon Wilders? Did you find out any more about them?'

Will paused, his foot on the pedal.

'Yes,' he said, 'there was a tale in the Middle Ages that some of them practised something called lycanthropy.'

'Lycanthropy? But that's –'

'And there was one who lived in Saxon times – he was known as Wandering Will. He was supposed to come back every twenty years – to see how his descendants were getting on. And when he came back –'

'Oh dear, there's my phone,' said the doctor. 'Just a minute. Don't go yet, Will.'

But when the doctor returned from answering the phone, Will had cycled away.

'I wonder if he'll take his bike to Canada?' the doctor thought, looking after him.

*

Will did; the great plains of northern Canada are wide and flat, endless pine forest and corn prairie, corn prairie and pine forest, through which the roads, straight as knives, run on seemingly for ever; wonderful roads they are for cycling, though you seldom see a cyclist on them. People stared in amazement to see the little dot that was Will come pedalling over the horizon, on and on across that huge flatness, sometimes under the broiling sun, sometimes in a fierce wind that had swept straight down from the North Pole.

Will was so quiet and serious, so straightforward and

eager after knowledge, that people everywhere were ready to answer his questions. Yes, there were still wolves in the woods; yes, the Indians still believed that if you trod on a wolf's footprint you were drawn after him and must follow him helplessly day and night through the forest. And there were wolves in the prairie too, the Indians thought; when a wave of wind passed over those great inland seas of maize or wheat they would say, 'Look, a wolf is running through the corn!' and they believed that when the last sheaf was harvested, the wolf who was hiding in it must be caught, or there would be no grain harvest next year.

Did the wolves ever attack people? Will asked. Opinions were divided on that; some said yes, wolves would follow a sleigh all day, and pounce on the travellers when dark came; others said no, wolves seldom or never harmed a man but preyed only on small game, rabbits, chipmunks, or woodmice.

So Will went on, and at last he came to the town of Wilderness, which stood beyond the forest, on the edge of a great frozen swamp. Its wooden frame houses were so old, so grey, that they looked more like piles of lichen than human dwellings; not many people lived here now, and all the ones who did were old; they sat on their weathered porches in the sun all summer long, and in rocking-chairs by large log fires through the winter.

Will asked if Mrs Smith lived here still. No, somebody said, she died last winter. But, yes, old Barney Davies was still alive; he lived in the last house on the left, before the forest began.

So Will went to call on old Barney Davies; a little shrunken wisp of a man, as weathered and grey as his house. He sat by a pine-knot fire, over which Will heated a can of beans that he took from his pack.

'Yes,' said old Barney, eating his share of the beans,

'your grandfather used to live here. A quiet fellow he was, come from farther east. And his son, your father, yes, he lived here too, married Mary Smith and they went off saying they'd be back. But they never came back. Your grandfather died a couple of years after they left. Friend of mine, he was. I've a few of his things still, if you'd like to see them.'

'I'd like to very much,' said Will, making coffee in an old kerosene tin. So Barney Davies rummaged in a wooden chest and presently brought out a rope of Indian beads and a tobacco pouch and a mildewed leather belt and a small oilskin bag which held a wad of old, yellowed linen folded so damp and flat that Will had trouble prising it apart.

'Did my grandfather come from England?' he asked, holding the wad near the fire to dry it.

'Never said. Maybe he did. Never let on. Used to talk about England some. Made a living mending folks' pots and pans. A rare clever hand he was at that.'

'What else did he do?'

'Used to spend a lot of time in the woods. Whole days, weeks together he'd be away. Not hunting or trapping. Never brought anything back. Seemed as if he was searching for something he never found.'

By now Will had got the linen a bit dried and, very slowly, with infinite care, he unfolded it.

'Kind of an old map?' said Barney Davies, taking the pipe from his mouth. 'Nowhere round here, though, I reckon.'

'No,' Will said, 'it's an English map.'

Ye Wildernesse of Whorplesdene, said the aged script across the top of the mildewed sheet. A river ran across the middle, the River Wey. Pine forests were drawn in one corner, ash forests in another. Camp, it said, between the pine forest and the ash. Norman Village, in another corner. Pitch kettles, charcoal fire. And, crossways, a path seemed to be marked. By straining his eyes, Will thought he could just make out the inscription along the path – which seemed, as far as he could judge, to follow the track now taken by the main line from Woking to Guildford: he read the name aloud.

'Wandering Will's Way.'

'Wandering Will,' said old Barney. 'I mind your grandfather talking about him.'

'What did he say?'

'The Indians believe in something called the Wendigo,' old Davies said. 'Half man, half wolf. Runs through the forest. When you hear him, you have to follow. Or if you tread on his footprint, or if he crosses your track. Wandering Will was the same sort of critter, I reckon, only back in England. When he takes hold of you, he gives you a kind of longing for places where folk have never been, for things nobody knows.'

'Yes I see.'

'Want to keep the map?'

'May I?'

'Sure. It's properly yours. Well,' said old Barney, 'guess it's time for me to have my nap. Nice meeting you. So long, young fellow. Be going back to England now, I reckon?'

'Quite soon,' said Will. He put the map carefully in his pocket, mounted his bike, and rode away along the road that skirted between forest and swamp.

He reckoned that before nightfall he ought to be able to reach the next town, Moose Neck, forty miles farther on.

But he reckoned without the weather.

In mid afternoon a few flakes of snow began to fall, and by dusk they had increased to a blizzard. Will did not dare continue cycling, he could not see ahead; there was nothing to prevent his going straight into the swamp, or into the river that crossed it.

He dismounted, tightened the strings of his Parka, wrapped his waterproof cape round him, and huddled under the shelter of a spruce tree. Colder and colder it grew, darker and darker. The wind wailed through the forest like a banshee, like a mourning dragon, like a pack of starved dinosaurs. But in spite of the wind's roar, Will found it hard to keep his eyes open.

'I mustn't go to sleep,' he thought. 'To sleep in this would be certain death. But I'm so tired – so tired . . . I shall have to go to sleep . . .'

His eyes closed . . .

It seemed to him that he was not alone. All about him he could feel the nearness of live creatures, feel movement and stirring and warm breath. It seemed to him that he opened his eyes and saw many pairs of green lights, shining luminous in the dark; he knew they were the eyes of wolves. He could feel fur, and the warmth of bodies pressed tight against him.

'Don't be afraid,' their voices were telling him. 'Don't be afraid, we are your friends.'

'I'm not afraid,' Will said truly. 'But why are you my friends? Most men are afraid of you.'

'We are your friends because you are part of our family. You are the boy with a wolf's foot.'

'Yes, that is true,' said Will in his dream.

'You do not belong here, though. You must go back to the place you came from; you will not get what you are seeking here.'

'What am I seeking?' Will asked.

'You will know when you find it.'

'Where shall I find it?'

'In your own place, where the wolves hunt no longer, save in dreams, or in memory, or in thought, or in fear.

In your own corner of your own land, where your forefathers were friends to wolves, where your cradle lay across the wolf's path. You must go back. You must go back.'

'Yes,' said Will in his sleep. 'I must go back.'

He sank deeper into warmth and darkness.

When he next opened his eyes, a dazzling sun was rising over the swamp. No wolves were to be seen; but all round the spruce tree were the prints of paws like dogs' paws, only bigger; a tuft of grey fur had lodged under a flap of Will's Parka. He tucked it between the folds of his map of Worplesdon Wilderness.

Then, through the loose, soft new snow he bicycled on to Moose Neck.

*

When Will returned to England, he caught the 18.06 stopping train from Waterloo to Guildford. He got out at Worplesdon, left the station, climbed over a fence, and limped back along beside the track until he came to a piece of waste-land, dotted all over with clumps of bramble, and with piles of bricks and stacks of old timber.

Then he sat himself down on the embankment beside a clump of willow, and waited.

It was dark. The wind was rising.

Presently he felt a puff of cold air on his cheek, and heard a voice in his ear.

'Well, my child? Finding me took you long enough, and far enough! Now you have found me at last, what do you want?'

'I'm not certain,' said Will. 'When I was younger I always wanted one thing – to be able to run faster than a train. But now – I'm not sure. I seem to want so many different things.'

'Well, think carefully! If you wanted it, I could take

away your wolf's foot; I could help you run faster than a train. Do you want to try?'

It seemed to Will that the cold wind caught him by the arms; he was running along the grassy embankment – fast, faster – black air and signal lights streamed past him, there was a black-and-gold ribbon ahead of him; he caught up and overtook the 22.50 from Waterloo and raced into Guildford ahead of it. Then the wind swung him round and took him back to where he had been before.

'That was wonderful!' Will gasped, grabbing the old willow to steady himself. 'But I know now that it's not what I want. I want to learn, I want to find out hundreds of things. Can you help me do that?'

'Yes, I can help you! Goodbye then, my child. You won't see me again, but I shall be with you very often.'

'Good-bye, great-grandfather,' said Will.

*

Dr Talisman was sitting late in his study, writing up his notes on the day's cases, when he heard his bell ring. He went to the door.

'Will! So you're back from Canada! It's good to see you – come and have some coffee.'

'It's good to be back.' Will limped into the doctor's study.

'So – did you hear many legends about wolves?'

'Yes I did,' said Will. 'And some true tales too.'

'And did you find the town where your father had lived?'

'Yes, I found it.'

'By the way,' Dr Talisman said, 'Moberley thinks he can operate on that foot of yours and cure your lameness; make you the same as everybody else.'

'That's kind of him,' said Will, 'but I've decided I don't want an operation. I'd rather keep my foot the way it is.'

'Are you quite sure?' said the doctor, somewhat astonished. 'Well – you know your own mind, I can see. And have you decided on a career?'

'Yes,' Will said. 'I'm going to be a doctor, like you – Oh, I think this is yours: I found it tonight.'

And he handed the doctor a tarnished old watch that looked as if it had been buckled round the branch of a tree for twenty years.

Mrs Nutti's Fireplace

MARK, who wished to get rid of the space-gun his great-uncle had sent him, and acquire something more useful, had brought home a copy of *Exchange and Mart*.

'"Princess-type boiler fireplace exchanged for gent's bicycle,"' he read aloud consideringly.

'But we don't want a fireplace,' Harriet pointed out. 'And we haven't a bicycle.'

'Or there's five gross jazz-coloured balloons, a tiger's head, and two whale teeth. Offered in exchange for go-kart or griffin's eggs.'

'The balloons would be nice.' Harriet swallowed her last bite of cake – they were having Friday tea – and came to hang over his shoulder. 'If we had a go-kart.'

'"Sale or exchange road-breaker tools interested arc welder, spray plant, w.h.y. Buyer collects." I do wonder w.h.y. ? They seem queer things to collect.'

'"Pocket Gym, judo suit, height increaser, neck developer, strength course, weights, and Dynamic Tension course." *That* seems a bargain. Only three pounds.'

'No height increasers in this family, thanks,' said Mr Armitage, without looking up from his evening paper. 'Or weight increasers. Kindly remember the house is three hundred years old.'

'"A hundredweight of green garnishing in 10-inch sections, de-rinder and sausage-spooling machinery"; they might come in handy for Christmas decorations,' Harriet said thoughtfully.

'"One million toys at 65p per 100, including Woo-Woos, Jumping Shrimp, et cetera."'

'Mother wouldn't like the Jumping Shrimp.'

'I would not,' agreed Mrs Armitage, pouring herself another cup of tea.

'*Gosh*! "7 in. span baboon spider with ½in. fangs, £5."'

'*No.*'

'I don't really want it,' Harriet said hastily. 'But – listen – "2½-year-old Himalayan bears, only £42" – oh, mother, *they'd* be lovely. "Or would exchange griffin's eggs." What a pity we haven't any of those. Lots of people seem to want them.'

'*Forty-two pounds*? You can't be serious. Besides, it would be too warm for Himalayan bears here.'

'"Various rattlesnakes, 6 ft Mangrove snake, £8."'

'Shall we get away from this section?' Mr Armitage suggested, lowering his paper. 'Anyway, isn't it time for your music lesson, Mark?'

'Yes, in just a minute. Here's something that might interest Mr Johansen,' Mark said. '"Would exchange room in town for room in country; pleasant outlook required. View by appointment." Mr Johansen was saying only last week that he wished he had a bedsit in London so that he could go to concerts and not always have to miss the last movement to catch the ten-fifteen. I'll take this along to show him.'

'Bring it back, though,' said Harriet, who did not want to lose track of the Himalayan bears.

Mark was very fond of Mr Johansen his music teacher, a sad, gentle man who, as well as teaching the piano and violin, had for many years run a dogs' weekend guest house. Lately, however, he had given up the dogs because he said he was growing too old to exercise them properly. When young, he had been in love with a German princess who had been lost to him by an unfortunate bit of amateur magic. He had never married. Everybody in the village liked him very much.

'Look, Mr Johansen,' said Mark, before settling down

to his five-finger exercises. 'You were saying only the other day that it was a pity not to use your spare room; here's somebody who wants to exchange a room in town for one in the country. Don't you think that would do for you?'

'Ach, so?' Mr Johansen carefully scanned the advertisement. 'Why yes, ziss might certainly be useful. I wvonder wvere ziss room is? I will write off to ze box number.' He made a note of it.

A week passed. Harriet, who had developed a passionate wish for a Himalayan bear, was hardly seen; she spent every evening making very beautiful dolls' furniture out of egg-shells, plastic egg-boxes, yoghurt pots, snail shells, and shampoo containers; when she had a hamper full of furniture she hoped to sell it all to a London toyshop for the price of a bear. She had not mentioned this plan to Mrs Armitage, who thought that a cat and a unicorn were sufficient pets for one family.

'Candleberry's lovely to ride on,' Harriet said to Mark, 'but you can't bring him indoors. And Walrus is always out catching mice. A bear would be cosy.'

Mark was in the middle of his lesson with Mr Johansen the following week when there came a brisk peal at the front-door bell. The music master opened the door and let in an uncommon-looking old lady, very short, very wrinkled, rather like a tortoise with a disagreeable expression, wearing rimless glasses and a raincoat and sou'-wester which might have been made of alligator-skin. She limped, and walked with a stick, and carried a carpet-bag which seemed to be quite heavy.

'Answer to advertisement,' she said in a businesslike manner. 'Name, Mrs Nutti. Room in town exchange room in country. Which room? This one?'

She stumped into the music-room. Mark twirled round on his music-stool to look at her.

'No, no. Upstairs,' said Mr Johansen. 'Ziss way, if you please.'

'Good. Upstairs better. Much better. Better outlook. Air fresher. Burglars not so likely. Can't do with burglars – Well, show way, then!'

Mr Johansen went ahead, she followed, Mark came too.

The music teacher's house was really a bungalow, and the spare room was really an attic-loft, with sloping ceilings. But it had big dormer windows with a pleasant view of fields and woods; Mr Johansen had painted the walls (or ceiling) sky blue, so that you could imagine you were out on the roof, rather than inside a room; there was blue linoleum on the floor, an old-fashioned bed with brass knobs and a patchwork quilt, and an even older-fashioned wash-stand with a jug and basin covered in pink roses.

'Very nice,' said Mrs Nutti looking round. 'Very nice view. Take it for three months. Beginning now.'

'But wait,' objected Mark, seeing that Mr Johansen was rather dazed by this rapid dealing. '*He* hasn't seen *your* room yet. And shouldn't you exchange references or something? I'm sure people always do that.'

'References?' snapped Mrs Nutti. 'No point. Not exchanging references – exchanging rooms! You'll find my room satisfactory. Excellent room. Show now.'

She snapped her fingers. Mark and Mr Johansen both lost their balance, as people do in a fairground trick room with a tilting floor, and fell heavily.

Mark thought as he fell,

'That's funny, I'd have said there was lino on this floor, not carpet.'

'Donnerwetter!' gasped Mr Johansen (Mark had fallen on top of him). They clambered to their feet, rather embarrassed.

'It is zose heavy lorries,' the music master began explaining apologetically. 'Zey do shake ze house so when zey pass; but is not so very often –'

Then he stopped, staring about him in bewilderment, for Mrs Nutti was nowhere to be seen.

Nor, for that matter, was the brass-headed bed, the patchwork quilt, the wash-stand with jug and roses, the blue ceiling –

'Gosh,' said Mark. He crossed to one of two high, latticed casement windows, treading noiselessly on the thick carpet, which was intricately patterned in red, blue, rose-colour, black, and gold. '*Gosh*, Mr Johansen, do come and look out.'

The music master joined him at the window and they gazed together into a city filled with dusk, whose lights were beginning to twinkle out under a deep-blue, clear sky with a few matching stars. Below them, a street ran downhill to a wide river or canal; a number of slender towers, crowned with onion-shaped domes, rose in every direction; there were masts of ships on the water and the cries of gulls could be heard.

Immediately below there was a small cobbled square and, on the opposite side of it, a café with tables set under a big leafy tree which had lights strung from its branches. A group of men with odd instruments – long curving pipes, bulb-shaped drums, outsize jews' harps – were playing a plaintive tune, while another man went round among the tables, holding out a wooden bowl.

'I do not understand,' muttered Mr Johansen. 'Wvat has happened? Wvere are we? Wvere is Mrs Nutti? *Wvere is my room*?'

'Why, don't you see, sir,' said Mark, who, more accustomed to this kind of thing, was beginning to guess what had happened. 'This must be Mrs Nutti's room that she said she'd show you. I thought she meant in London but of course in the advertisement it didn't actually say

London it just said 'room in town' – I wonder what town this is?'

'But – ach, himmel – zen wvere is *my* room?'

'Well, I suppose Mrs Nutti has got it. This seems quite a nice room, though, don't you think?'

Mr Johansen gazed about it rather wildly, pushing long thin hands through his white hair until the strands were all standing on end and he looked like a gibbon.

Mrs Nutti's room was furnished in a much more stately way than the humble attic bedroom. For a start, there was a massive four-poster bed with crimson damask hangings. The walls, also, were covered with some kind of damask, which made the room rather dark. Two tall black polished cabinets on claw feet stood against the wall facing the windows. A lamp in a boat-shaped gilt container hung suspended by a chain from the ceiling and threw a dim light. A velvet curtain, held back by a tasselled cord, partly covered the doorway; a small organ stood to the right of the door. Strangest of all, opposite the doorway there was a fireplace with a large heavy pair of polished metal andirons and a massive white marble mantelpiece which appeared to have suffered from some accident. The right side of the mantel was supported by a large carved marble heraldic beast with a collar round its neck, but the beast that should have supported the left-hand side was missing; it had apparently been dragged out of the wall, like a decoration from an iced cake, leaving nothing but a jagged hole.

'*That*'s a bit of a mess,' Mark said. 'I do think Mrs Nutti should have put it right for you before she lent you her room. It's rather a shame; the monster on the other is awfully nice. A kind of furry eagle.'

'A griffin,' corrected Mr Johansen absently. 'Ze legs, you see, are zose of a lion. Head, zat of an eagle, also wvings. But wvere *is* zis Mrs Nutti?'

'Wherever she is, she's left her carpet-bag behind,' said Mark, picking it off the floor. 'Blimey, what a weight. Hey, Mrs Nutti? Are you downstairs?'

He put the bag down again, walked through the open door, and stuck his head back through again to say, 'She really has done a neat job, Mr Johansen, it's still your landing outside.'

Bemusedly, Mr Johansen followed him out and discovered that, as Mark had said, the transformation of the loft-room went no farther than the door; outside were Mr Johansen's tidy bare landing, his coconut-matted stairs, and his prints of Alpine flora.

They went down, expecting to find Mrs Nutti in the music room. But she had gone.

'Back to wherever she came from, I suppose,' Mark said.

'Taking my room wizz her,' Mr Johansen murmured plaintively.

'But really, sir, hers is quite a nice room, don't you think? And it has a smashing view. I know it's not London, which was what you wanted, but maybe they have concerts in this town too. Where do you suppose it is?'

'How should I know?' said poor Mr Johansen, twisting his hair some more.

'Do let's go back upstairs and have another look.'

But by the time they had gone back, full dark had fallen on the town outside the window of the new room, and not much could be seen except a wide prospect of twinkling lights. They could hear music from across the square, and smell delicious smells of herbs and grilled meat.

'We'll have to come back in daylight,' Mark suggested. 'Tell you one thing, though, this place must be east of England; it gets dark sooner.'

'Zat is so,' agreed Mr Johansen. 'In any case, I suppose

zose towers are minarets; zis town is perhaps in Turkey or Persia.'

'What's Turkish music like, is it nice? Shall we have a wander round the streets and ask where the place is?'

Mr Johansen was somewhat hesitant about this; it took Mark a while to persuade him.

But now they came up against a difficulty: they could see the town, but there seemed to be no way of getting into it. If they went downstairs and out through Mr Johansen's front door, they merely found themselves in his ordinary garden, walking between neat rows of Canterbury bells towards the commonplace village street.

'We'll have to jump out of the window,' Mark said.

But it was a very much higher drop from Mrs Nutti's window – and on to a cobbled street at that – than from Mr Johansen's attic. Mr Johansen demurred.

'Never should I be able to face your dear Muzzer if you wvere to break your leg. Besides, how should wve get back?'

Mark had not considered this problem.

'I'll bring our fruit-ladder from home tomorrow morning,' he said. 'Perhaps I'd better be off now; Mother gets worried if I'm more than three-quarters of an hour late for supper, and thinks I've fallen in a river or something.'

Harriet was greatly interested in the story of Mr Johansen's room-exchange.

'I wonder *why* Mrs Nutti wanted to swap?' she pondered, and made Mark tell her over and over the few not particularly enlightening things the old lady had said.

'She seemed worried about burglars? And part of the fireplace was missing? Perhaps burglars had gone off with it?'

'You'd hardly think anyone would pinch half a fireplace,' Mark objected. 'Still, it was gone, that's true. Maybe she wanted to make sure no one could go off with the other half.'

'What was in the carpet-bag she left behind? Did you look? Do you think she left it by mistake or on purpose?'

'I didn't look. It was jolly heavy, whatever it was. Maybe she got fed up with carrying it about.'

'When you go down tomorrow I'm coming too,' Harriet said firmly.

'Good, then you can help carry the ladder.'

Taking the ladder was a waste of time, however, as they soon discovered. They leaned it up against the front of the house, so that its narrow top was wedged firmly against what appeared to be the window of Mr Johansen's attic.

Then they rang the door-bell and the music master let them in.

'Is the room still there, sir? Has Mrs Nutti been back? Did she fetch her bag? Can you still see the city?'

'Ja – ja – ze room is still zere, and ze bag also. But Frau Nutti has not returned. You wvish to see it?' he asked Harriet kindly.

'Oh yes, please!'

Mark and Harriet ran eagerly upstairs, Mr Johansen following more slowly.

'There!' said Mark with pride, pointing to the view.

'Coo!' breathed Harriet, taking it all in.

It was blazing daylight now, and obviously hot, hot weather, most unlike the grey chilly June day they had left behind downstairs. Dogs lay panting in the shade under the big tree. Men in caps like chopped-off cones sat sipping coffee and cool drinks. Boats with coloured sails plied to and fro across the river.

'What a gorgeous place,' said Harriet. 'Do let's go down. *Oh* – where's the ladder?'

'Not there,' said Mark sadly.

'What a swindle. I've an idea though – next time we

come we'll bring a rope. Then we can tie it to the window-catch and climb down.'

Mark cheered up at this practical plan. 'It's bad luck about your concerts, though, sir; still, I suppose it's only for three months.'

'Is no matter. I can listen to zose men across ze square; zeir music is most uncommon. Also I have ze organ to play on.'

He sat down at the little organ, fiddled around with bellows and pedals, and suddenly produced a short, sweet, powerful snatch of melody.

'Oh, do go on!' cried Harriet, as he stopped.

But he, looking round, said, 'Wvat wvas zat noise?'

A kind of crack or tap had come from the other side of the four-poster. Harriet ran round.

'It sounded like an electric bulb going. Oh, is this Mrs Nutti's bag? Heavens, it's heavy – whatever can there be in it?'

Harriet parted the flaps of the bag, which was not fastened, and began lifting out masses of empty paper bags, crumpled old magazines, chocolate wrappers, squashed cereal packets, newspapers, tissues, paper napkins, and other wadding.

'What a lot of junk. There's something hard and heavy right at the bottom though – quite big, too. Oh, it's an egg.'

Mr Johansen got up from the organ-stool and came to look over their shoulders at the contents of the carpet-bag.

An egg it certainly was, and no common egg either. It was a good deal bigger than a rugby ball; it might just have fitted into the oval kind of washing-up bowl. It was plain white, but veined over with faint greenish-blue lines. Egg-shaped.

'How queer that Mrs Nutti should have forgotten

about it –' Harriet was beginning, when the sound came from the egg again – crack!

'It's hatching!'

At this, Mr Johansen suddenly became very upset.

'No, no, zis I cannot have. Zis is too much! Her room, yes, I do not object, provided she take goot care of my room, I wvill do ze same for hers. But to have care of an egg, no, no, zat is ze outside, das tut mir zehr leid, I am not an incubator! Ze doggies I haf give up, because I can no longer take sufficient care –'

'I'll hatch it, I'll look after it!' said Harriet eagerly. 'I've hatched lots of owls' eggs, I'll put it in our airing-cupboard, I'll really look after it carefully, Mr Johansen. I'm sure Mother won't mind. Oh, do you suppose it could be a roc?'

'Not big enough,' said Mark.

Mr Johansen looked doubtful and distressed. 'Suppose Frau Nutti come back? It is, after all, her egg?'

'Then you tell her to come up the road to us,' Mark said. 'My sister really knows a lot about eggs, sir, she's an expert chick-raiser.'

'In zat case, best to get it home before it hatches quite out, nicht wahr?'

This proved a difficult task. The carpet-bag was so heavy that it took all their united strength to get it down the stairs.

'And you say Mrs Nutti was a little old lady?' said Harriet, scarlet with effort. 'How can she ever have carried it all the way from –'

'All the way from wherever she came from?'

'Well, we certainly can't carry it from here to home. Mr Johansen, could we possibly borrow your wheel-barrow?'

'Jawohl, yes indeed,' said Mr Johansen, only too glad to be rid of the responsibility of the egg before it hatched.

They balanced the fruit-ladder across the barrow and put the carpet-bag on top of the ladder, and so set off for home. Mr Johansen watched them anxiously until they were out of sight; then he started upstairs, going slowly at first but faster and faster. He entered Mrs Nutti's room, sat down at the organ, and was soon lost, deaf, and regardless of anything but the beautiful music he was making.

When Harriet and Mark reached the Armitage house and unloaded the carpet-bag, they were disconcerted to find that the egg's weight had bent the ladder into a V like a hockey-stick.

'Oh, dear,' Harriet said. 'I'm afraid Father's not going to be very pleased.'

Luckily their parents were out, so they were able to manhandle the egg upstairs without interference. A cast-iron cannon ball would not have been much harder to deal with.

'What kind of bird can it possibly be?' panted Harriet.

Mark had a theory, but he wasn't going to commit himself just yet.

'Maybe it comes from some planet where the atmosphere is less dense. Anyway, whatever it is, it seemed to enjoy Mr Johansen's music. Perhaps we ought to play to it, to help it hatch.'

'No organ, though; it'll have to be satisfied with recorders.'

The egg took longer to hatch than they had expected; perhaps the recorder music was not so stimulating. A couple of weeks went by. Occasional cracking noises came from the airing-cupboard, but Harriet had carefully swathed the egg in winter blankets, so that it was not visible; Mrs Armitage said absently, 'I do hope the immersion heater isn't going to blow up again,' but she was busy making strawberry jam and did not investigate the noises. 'Why have you children taken to playing your recorders on the upstairs landing all day long? Can't you find anything better to do?'

'Rehearsing for the fête,' Harriet said promptly.

'It seems a funny place to rehearse.'

'Well, it's warm, you see – just by the airing cupboard.'

At last the egg burst.

'Good god, what's that?' said Mr Armitage, rushing in from the garden, where he had been thinning out lettuces.

'Oh my gracious, do you think someone's planted a bomb on us?' exclaimed his wife, dropping a pot of jam on the kitchen floor.

'More likely something those children have been up to,' said their loving father.

Mark and Harriet had been eating their elevenses – apples and cheese – in the playroom.

At the tremendous bang they looked at each other with instantaneous comprehension of what had happened, and raced upstairs.

'Heavens! The smell!' gasped Harriet.

It was very strong.

'Sulphur,' said Mark knowledgeably.

There was a good deal of mess about, too. The airing-cupboard door was a splintered wreck, and the floor and walls for some distance round were splashed with yellow goo, like egg-yolk, only more so. Several windows were cracked.

A tangle of damp and soggy blankets and towels on the upstairs landing made it difficult to get to the airing-cupboard.

Mr and Mrs Armitage arrived.

'What *happened*?' cried Mrs Armitage.

'Harriet put an egg to hatch in the airing-cupboard,' Mark explained.

'An egg? What kind of an egg, would you be so kind as to explain?'

'Well, we don't know yet – somebody left it with Mr Johansen, you see, and he didn't feel quite equal to the worry –'

'Oh, delightful,' said Mr Armitage. 'So he just passed it on to us. Mr Johansen is an excellent music teacher but I really –'

'Listen!' said Harriet.

From the sodden mass of household linen still inside the cupboard came a plaintive sound.

It was a little like the call of a curlew – a kind of thin, bubbling, rising, sorrowful cry.

'It's the chick!' exclaimed Harriet joyfully, and she began pulling out pillowcases and tablecloths. Out with them came the lower half of Mrs Nutti's egg, and, still crouched in it, filling it and bulging over the broken edges, they saw a bedraggled, crumpled, damp, dejected creature that seemed all bony joints and big eyes and limp horny claws.

'Well – it's rather a poppet,' Harriet said, after a pause.

Mr Armitage stared at it and made a thoughtful comment. 'I'm not a one for rash statements, but I don't think I *ever*, in all my born days, laid eyes on an uglier, scrawnier, soggier, more repulsive-looking chick. In the north country they'd call it a bare golly. What's it supposed to be, tell me that?'

'And for this hideous monster,' wailed Mrs Armitage, 'all our sheets and blankets and tablecloths and the best monogrammed towels have to be ruined?'

'Honestly, Ma, don't worry,' Harriet said. 'Mark and I will take everything down to the coin-op dry-clean after lunch, I promise. I must just give the chick a rinse first, and set him on the playroom radiator to dry. You'll see, when he's cleaned up and fluffed out he'll look quite different.'

'He can look a whole lot different and still be as ugly as sin,' prophesied Mr Armitage.

'And what's he going to eat?' demanded Mrs Armitage, as Harriet lifted up the chick, egg-shell and all, and carried him away, staggering under his weight, to the playroom, calling to Mark over her shoulder as she did so to fetch a bucket of warm water and some soapless shampoo.

While they were cleaning and disinfecting the sheets and blankets at the laundromat (it took three trips and the whole afternoon and all their next month's allowance) Mark said to Harriet,

'Now do you know what the chick is?'

'No, but he's a very queer shape, I must say. His back end isn't a bit like a bird, and he's got a funny straggly tail with a tassel at the end. How big do you think he's likely to grow?'

'I should think he's about a fifth of his full size now.'

'How do you reckon that?'

'I think he's a griffin-chick.'

'A griffin?' said Harriet, dismayed. 'Are you sure?'

'Well, he's just like the one carved on Mrs Nutti's mantelpiece.'

'Oh my goodness,' Harriet said sadly. 'If only we'd known when he was in the egg, we could have exchanged him for a Himalayan bear.'

'No we couldn't,' said Mark primly. 'He's not ours to swap. He's Mrs Nutti's. I suppose she sent him to the country to hatch out.'

'Well, *I* think it was very neglectful of her to go off and just *leave* him.'

When they finally tottered home with the last piles of clean laundry ('Honestly,' grumbled Mark, 'we shall have biceps like boa-constrictors after all the lifting we've done lately,') Harriet's disappointment over the loss of the Himalayan bear was greatly reduced.

'Oh, I say!' she exclaimed, lifting a fold of newspaper in the laundry basket which they had left propped against the warm radiator. 'Do look! He's dried off and he's *furry*!'

At the sound of her voice the griffin-chick woke up, sleepily uncurled, and staggered out from among the crumpled newspapers.

His appearance was now quite different. The dark damp tendrils all over his back, sides, hind legs and tail were fluffed out into soft, thick grey fur, like that of a short-haired Persian cat. His stumpy little wings and head were covered with pale grey eiderdown. His beak, brown before, had turned red, and it was wide open.

'Gleep. Gleep. Thrackle, thrackle, thrackle. Gleep. GLEEP!'

'Oh, heavens, he's starving! Just a minute, Furry, hang on a tick, and we'll get you something to eat. Do you suppose he'll eat bread-and-milk?'

'We can try,' said Mark.

Bread-and-milk went down splendidly, when dolloped into the gaping red beak with a dessert-spoon. One basin-ful was not enough. Nor were two. Nor were seven. But after the ninth bowlful the baby griffin gave a great happy yawn, closed his beak and eyes simultaneously, clambered on to the lap of Harriet, who was kneeling on the floor beside him, tucked his head under a wing (from where it immediately slipped out again as the wing was not nearly big enough to cover it) and fell asleep.

After about three minutes Harriet said,

'It's like having a cart-horse on one's lap. I'll have to shift him.'

Struggling like a coal-heaver she shifted the chick on to the hearthrug. He did not even blink.

Harriet and Mark sat thoughtfully regarding their new acquisition.

'He's going to be expensive to feed,' Mark said.

This proved an understatement.

After three weeks Mrs Armitage said, 'Look, I don't want to seem mean, and I must admit your Furry does look better now he isn't so bony and goose-pimply but – thirty-six bowls of bread-and-milk a day!'

'Yes, it is a lot,' agreed Harriet sadly.

'Maybe Mr Johansen could contribute towards his support?'

'Oh, no, he's awfully hard up,' Mark said. 'I'll pay for the bread and Harriet can pay for the milk. I've some money saved from apple-picking.'

'That still leaves the sugar and raisins.'

Harriet decided that she would have to dispose of her dolls' furniture.

Unfortunately that was the day when Furry, tired of his newspaper nest, looked round for somewhere new to roost, and noticed the wicker hamper in which Harriet stored her finished products. He flapped his little wings, jumped up on top, turned round two or three times, digging his claws into the wicker, until he was comfortable, stuck his head under his wing (where it now fitted better; his wings were growing fast) and went to sleep. Slowly the hamper sagged beneath his weight; by the time Harriet found him it was completely flattened, like a wafer-ice that has been left in the sun.

'Oh, *Furry*! *Look* what you've done!'

'Gleep,' replied the baby griffin mournfully, stretching out first one hind leg and then the other.

He was hungry again.

'It's no use blaming him,' Harriet said, inspecting her ruined work. 'He just doesn't know his own weight.'

The next night was a chilly one, and in the middle of it Furry, becoming fretful and shivery and lonesome, clambered on to Harriet's bed for warmth and company. Harriet, fast asleep, began to have strange dreams of avalanches and earthquakes; by the morning three legs of her bed had buckled under Furry's weight; Furry and Harriet were huddled in a heap down at the south-west corner.

'It's queer,' said Mark, 'considering how fast he's putting on weight, that he doesn't grow very much bigger.'

'He's more condensed than we are,' Harriet said.

'Condensed!' said Mrs Armitage. 'From now on, that creature has got to live out of doors. Any day now he'll go right through the floorboards. And your father says the same.'

'Oh mother!'

'It's no use looking at *me* like that. Look at the play-room floor! It's sagging, and dented all over with claw-marks; it looks like Southend beach.'

'I suppose he'll have to roost in the woodshed,' Harriet said sadly.

They fetched a load of hay and made him a snug nest. While he was investigating it, and burying himself up to his beak, they crept indoors and went to bed, feeling like the parents of Hansel and Gretel.

Next morning Furry was up on the woodshed roof, gleeping anxiously. The woodshed had tilted over at a forty-five-degree angle.

'Oh, Furry! How did you ever get up there?'

'He must have flown,' said Mark.

'But he can't fly!'

'He was bound to start soon; his wings are nearly full-grown. And proper feathers are sprouting all over them, and on his head too.'

If Furry had flown up to the roof of the shed, however, he showed no signs of remembering how to set about flying down again. He teetered about on the sloping roof, gleeping more and more desperately. At last, just in time, he managed to fly a few hasty, panic-stricken flaps, and coasted to earth as the shed collapsed behind him.

'You *clever* baby,' said Harriet, giving him a hug to show that nobody blamed him.

'Thrackle, thrackle. Gleep, cooroocooroo, gleep.' Furry leaned lovingly against Harriet. She managed to leap aside just before he flattened her; he now weighed as much as a well-nourished grizzly.

Harriet and Mark were extremely busy. In order to earn Furry's keep they had taken jobs, deliving papers, selling petrol at the garage, and washing up at the Two-Door Café, but they were in a constant state of anxiety all the time as to what he might be doing while they were away from home.

'Do you think we ought to mention to Mr Johansen that it's rather difficult with Furry?' Harriet suggested one day. 'It isn't that I'm not *fond* of him –'

'It's rather difficult to get him to pay attention these days; Mr Johansen, I mean.'

Indeed, the music master seemed to be in a dream most of the time.

'Never haf I played such an instrument, never!' he declared. When he was not playing Mrs Nutti's organ he was leaning out of the spare-room window, gazing at the view, listening to the music across the square, rapt in a kind of trance. Mark was a little worried about him.

'Honestly, sir, don't you think you ought to get out for a bit of fresh air sometimes?'

'But you see I have ze feeling zat from zis window I might some day see my lost Sophie.'

'But even if you did, we still don't know how to get into the town.'

Their experiment with rope had proved a failure. The rope had simply disappeared, as fast as they paid it out of the window. Nor was it possible to attract the attention of the people down below and persuade them to fetch a ladder (which had been another of Harriet's suggestions). Neither shouts nor waves had the slightest effect. And Mr Johansen had vetoed any notion of either Mark or Harriet climbing out.

'For you might disappear like ze rope, and zen what should I tell your dear Muzzer?'

'So even if you did see your lost Sophie from the window it wouldn't do you much good; it would be more of a worry than anything else,' Mark said with ruthless practicality.

'Ach – who knows – who knows?' sighed Mr Johansen.

Several more weeks passed. Furry, measured by Mark, was now nearly as big as the marble griffin under the mantelpiece.

Then, one evening, when Mark was in the midst of his piano lesson, Harriet burst in.

'Oh – Mr Johansen – I'm most terribly sorry to interrupt – but it's Furry! He's flown up on top of the water-tower, and he's dreadfully scared and gleeping away like mad, and I'm so afraid he might damage the tower – *do* come, Mark, and see if you can talk him down, you're the one he trusts most. I've brought a pail of bread-and-milk.'

They ran outside, Mr Johansen following. It was the first time he had been out for days.

The village water-tower stood a couple of fields away from the music master's bungalow. It was a large metal cylinder supported on four metal legs which looked slender to support the weight of goodness knows how many thousand gallons of water, but were apparently equal to the job. It did not, however, seem likely that they were equal to supporting a full-grown griffin as well, particularly since he was running back and forth on top of the cylinder, gleeping distractedly, opening and shutting his wings, leaning to look over the edge, and then jumping back with a tremendous clatter and scrape of toenails on galvanized iron.

'*Furry*!' shouted Mark. 'Keep calm! Keep calm!'

'Gleep! Thrackle, thrackle, thrackle.'

'Shut your wings and stand still,' ordered Mark.

With his eyes starting out as he looked at the awful drop below him, the griffin obeyed.

'Now, Harriet, swing the bucket of bread-and-milk round a bit, so the smell rises up.'

Harriet did so. Some bread-and-milk slopped out on the grass. The sweet and haunting fragrance steamed up through the evening air.

'Gleeeeeep!'

A famished wail came from the top of the water-tower.

'You're very silly!' Harriet shouted scoldingly. 'If you hadn't got yourself up there you could be eating this nice bread-and-milk now.'

'Furry,' called Mark, 'watch me. Are you watching?'

Silence from up above. Then a faint thrackle.

'Right! Now, open your wings.'

Mark had his arms by his sides; he now raised them to shoulder height.

Furry, after a moment or two, hesitantly did the same.

'Now lower them again. Do as I do. Just keep raising and lowering.'

Following Mark's example, Furry did this half a dozen times. The tower shook a bit.

'Right, faster and faster. Faster still! Now – *jump*! KEEP FLAPPING!'

Furry jumped, and forgot to flap; he started falling like a stone.

'Gleep!'

'*Flap*, you fool!'

The onlookers leapt away; just in time, Furry began flapping again and, when he was within eight feet of the ground, suddenly soared upwards once more.

'*Don't* land on the tower again. Flap with *both* wings – not just one. You're going ROUND AND ROUND,' Mark shouted, cupping hands about his mouth. 'That's better. Don't flap so fast. Slower! Like this!'

He demonstrated.

Furry hurtled past, eyes tight shut, claws clenched, wings nothing but a blur. Then back again. It was like the progress of a balloon with the string taken off.

'Make your strokes *slower*.'

'It's as bad as learning to swim,' Harriet said. 'People get quick and frantic in just the same way. Still, he is doing better now. Just so long as he doesn't hit the tower. Or Mr Johansen's roof.'

Several times Furry had only just cleared the bungalow. At last, more or less in control, he flapped himself down to Mr Johansen's front garden, shaving off all the front hedge on his way, and flattening a bed of Canterbury bells.

Mark and Harriet arrived at top speed, with the half-full bucket slopping between them, and set it down on the path. Furry, gleeping between mouthfuls, began frantically gobbling.

At this rather distracted moment, Mrs Nutti arrived.

'What's this, then, what's this?' she snapped angrily, taking in the scene at a glance. 'Who let him out? Should be *upstairs*, in room, not in garden. Burglars, burglars might come, might see him.'

'Out?' said Harriet. 'He's too heavy to keep indoors these days.'

'All wrong – very bad,' said Mrs Nutti furiously. 'Why did I take room in country? To keep him out of way of griffin collectors. Town full of them. Come along, you!'

she bawled at Furry. Before Mark or Harriet could protest she had snapped a collar on his neck and dragged him indoors, up Mr Johansen's staircase.

They ran after her.

'Hey, stop!' shouted Mark. 'What are you doing with him?'

Arriving in the spare room, they found Mrs Nutti struggling to push Furry into the ragged hole under the mantelpiece.

'You don't mean', gasped Harriet, outraged, 'that you intend him to spend the rest of his life *there*, holding up that shelf?'

'Why else leave egg here to hatch?' panted Mrs Nutti angrily, dragging on the collar.

But Furry, reared on freedom and bread-and-milk, was too strong for Mrs Nutti.

With a loud snap the collar parted as he strained away from her, and he shot across the room, breaking one of the bedposts like a stick of celery. The window splintered as he struck it, and then he was out and away, flapping strongly up into the blue, blue star-sprinkled sky over the foreign city.

One gleep came back to them, then a joyful burst of the full, glorious song of an adult griffin.

Then he dwindled to a speck and was gone.

'There!' said Harriet. 'That just serves you right, Mrs Nutti. Why, you hadn't even looked after him and you expected him to hold up your fireplace!'

She was almost crying with indignation.

Mrs Nutti spoke to no one. With her lips angrily compressed she snatched up the carpet-bag, cast a furious look round the room, and marched out, pulling the room together behind her as one might drag along a counterpane.

By the time they heard the front door slam, they were

back in Mr Johansen's attic, with its brass bedstead and patchwork quilt.

Mr Johansen walked slowly to the window and looked out, at the trampled garden and the empty bread-and-milk bucket, which still lay on the path.

'I suppose we'll never see Furry again,' Mark said, clearing his throat.

'Or I, my Sophie,' sighed Mr Johansen.

'Oh, I don't know,' Harriet said. 'I wouldn't be surprised if Furry found his way back sometime. He's awfully fond of us. And I'm *sure* you'll find your Sophie some day, Mr Johansen. I really am sure you will.'

'We'll start looking for another room in town for you right away!' Mark called back, as they walked out through the battered gate.

'It really is lucky Furry didn't hit the water-tower,' Harriet said. 'I should think it would have taken years of pocket-money to pay for *that* damage. Now – as soon as we've fixed up the airing-cupboard door –'

'– And the fruit-ladder –'

'And the woodshed and the legs of my bed and Mr Johansen's front gate – I can start saving up for a Himalayan bear.'

Hope

It was on a clear, frosty November evening, not many years ago, that Doctor Jane Smith, having occasion to visit a patient in the part of London known as Rumbury Town, was suddenly overtaken by the impulse to call on an old teacher of hers, a Miss Lestrange, who had a bed-sitting-room on the edge of that district, where she earned a meagre living by giving lessons on the harp.

Rumbury Town is a curious region of London. Not far from the big stations, adjacent to Islington, beyond, or anyway defying the jurisdiction of smokeless-fuel legislation, it lies enfolded generally in an industrial dusk of its own. The factories of Rumbury Town are not large, and their products are eccentric – artificial grass for butchers' windows, metal bed-winches, false teeth for sheep, slimmers' biscuits made from wood-pulp, catnip mice, plastic Christmas-tree decorations – these are a random sample of its exports. But the small gaunt chimneys, leaning from the factories at various precarious angles, belch black smoke as vigorously as any modern electric power station, and so do those of the houses, like rows of organ-stops, along the ill-lit, dour little terraced streets that lead up in the direction of Rumbury Waste, the ragged strip of tree-grown land fringing Rumbury Town on its eastern edge.

Rumbury Waste is a savage place enough, on no account to be visited after dark, but many a police officer would agree that the centre of Rumbury Town itself is far more of a hostile wilderness, far more dangerous. Here lies an area of mixed factories, business premises, and

wholesale markets, interspersed with a few lanes of
private dwellings and some dingy little shopping pre-
cincts; seamed by narrow alleys and shortcuts; a real
maze where, it is said, only those born in Rumbury Town
or who have spent at least forty years within earshot of the
bells of St Griswold's, Rumbury, can ever hope to find
their way.

So cold and clear was this particular evening, however,
that even the smoke from the Rumbury chimneys had
dwindled to a slaty wisp against the sky's duck-egg green;
so little wind was there that in the derelict corners of
factory lots where goldenrod and willowherb cloaked
piles of rubble, the withered leaves and feathery seeds
drifted straight and unswerving to the ground.

Engines and presses in the factories had ceased their
clanging and thudding; workers had gone home; in the
centre of Rumbury Town the only sound to be heard was
the distant, muted roar of London; and a nearer surge
of pop music, sizzle of fish frying, and shouts of children
from the few inhabited streets. Dr Smith parked her car
in one of these, locked it carefully, and went in search of
her friend, Miss January Lestrange.

Rumbury Town seemed a curious environment for a
spinster who taught the harp. And Miss Lestrange was a
real spinster of the old-fashioned kind; she walked very
slowly, with small, precise steps; she wore tight, pointed
button boots, very shiny, which ended halfway up her
calf, and long serge skirts, trimmed with rows of braid,
which hung down over the boots; it was pure chance that
Miss Lestrange's style of dressing was now once more the
height of fashion, and a circumstance that she would
certainly not have noticed; had she done so she might have
been mildly irritated. Her grey hair was smoothly drawn
back into a bun, and she wore pince-nez; all the children
of Rumbury Town wondered how she managed to make

them balance on her nose. Miss Lestrange kept herself to herself and never troubled her neighbours; many of them, if they had thought about it, would not have been surprised to be told that she was a thin, grey old ghost, occasionally to be seen gliding out on her small shopping errands. And the children, though they were not exactly frightened of her, never chalked on her door, or threw ice-lolly sticks after her, or sang rude rhymes about her, as they did about most other adults in the neighbourhood. Miss Lestrange, however, was no ghost, and although she had lived within sound of St Griswold's bells for forty years, was not a born citizen of the district; she still did not venture into the twilit heart of Rumbury Town.

'Why *do* you live here?' Dr Smith asked, when she had knocked on the faded blue door with its postcard, J. LESTRANGE, HARP TUITION, and had been admitted, passing a small frantic-looking boy on his way out with a music-case under his arm.

'It amazes me the way some of them keep on coming,' murmured Miss Lestrange, zipping its case over the harp, which was as tall, gaunt and worn-looking as she herself. 'I've told them and told them that you don't get a first-rate harpist once in a generation, but they all think they have the seed of it in them.'

'What about that boy? Is he any good?'

Miss Lestrange shrugged.

'He's the same as the rest. I don't hold out false hopes and sweet promises. I send him away at the end of the lesson utterly despondent, limp as rhubarb, but by next time he's always plucked up heart again and thinks he'll be a second David. Well, Jane, it is nice to see you. What brings you here?'

'Suppose I said that *I* wanted some more lessons?' Dr Smith asked with a small, grim smile.

'I should tell you what I told your parents. It would be

a waste of their money, my time, and yours, to teach you for another five minutes.'

'And they at least believed you. So I went away and trained for a doctor.'

'And have turned into a good one, from what I hear.' Miss Lestrange nodded at her ex-pupil affectionately. 'I hope you will stay and take your evening meal with me and tell me about your work.'

But her glance strayed a little doubtfully to the screened corner of the room where she cooked over a methylated-spirit lamp; she had been about to brew herself a nourishing, or at least vitamin-rich soup, made from hot water, parsley, grown in her window-box, and salt.

'No, no, I came to invite you out. I have to pay one call on a patient not far from here, and then I thought we'd go to the Chinese Restaurant at the corner of Inkermann Street. Put on your coat and let's be off.'

Miss Lestrange was always businesslike.

'Well, that would certainly be a more enjoyable meal than the one I could have offered you,' she said, put on her coat, and a black hat which had the shape though not the festive air of a vol-au-vent, and ushered out her visitor, locking the door behind them.

The little grimy street was silent and watchful. Half a dozen children stared, to see Miss Lestrange setting out at such an unwonted time of day, in such an unwonted manner, in a car, with a friend.

Dr Smith reverted to her first, unanswered question.

'Why *do* you live here?'

'The rents are very low,' Miss Lestrange said mildly. 'Five pounds a year for my room.'

'But in a better part you might get more pupils – brighter ones . . .'

'The world is not that full of gifted harpists,' Miss Lestrange said drily. 'And this neighbourhood suits me.'

'You have friends here?'

'Once I did. One friend. We have not seen each other for some time. But as one grows older,' Miss Lestrange said calmly, 'one requires fewer friends.'

Reflecting that it would be difficult to have fewer friends than *one*, Dr Smith brought her car to a halt by a large, grim tenement with a dozen arched entrances. The road that passed it was an old, wide, cobbled one, and on the opposite side began the cluttered, dusky jumble of piled-up factory, warehouse, shed, storehouse, office, factory and lumber-yard that like a great human badger-warren covered the heart of Rumbury Town.

'My patient lives just through here; I shan't be long.'

'Who is your patient?' inquired Miss Lestrange, as the doctor turned to lift her black case from the rear seat of the car.

'Well, as a matter of fact he's quite well known – the writer Tom Rampisham. Why, like you, he chooses to live in this godforsaken spot I don't know, but here he's lived for goodness knows how many years. He has a ground-floor flat in that gloomy block.'

'Tom Rampisham,' Miss Lestrange said musingly. 'It is some time since he did one of his broadcasts. What's his trouble?'

'Heart. Well, I probably shan't be more than a few minutes. But here's a spare car-key in case you want to stroll about.'

It looked an unpromising area for a stroll. But when Dr Smith's few minutes lengthened to ten, and then to fifteen, Miss Lestrange, who seemed restless and disinclined to sit still, even after a long day's work, got out of the car, locked it, and stood irresolutely on the pavement.

For a moment she stared at the large forbidding block into which the doctor had vanished. Then, with decision, she turned her back on it and struck off briskly across the road. Almost immediately opposite the car was a little opening in the cliff-like façade of warehouses, one of those narrow lanes which the denizens of Rumbury Town call *hackets*, which led inwards, with many angles and windings and sudden changes of direction, towards the heart of the maze.

Along this alley Miss Lestrange rapidly walked. It seemed as if she walked *from* rather than *to* anything in particular; her head was bent, her eyes fixed on the greasy cobbles, she ignored the entrances with their mysterious signs: Wishaw, Flock Sprayers; Saloop, Ear Piercing Specialists; Ample Tops; The Cake Candle Co.; Madame Simkins, Feathers; Sugg, Ganister Maker and Refractory Materials Manufacturer; Toppling Seashell Merchants; Shawl, String, and Sheepskin Co.; Willow Specialists and Wood Wool Packers. One and all, she passed them without a glance, even the Shawl, String, and Sheepskin office, which was in fact the source of her new harp-strings when the old ones had snapped under the inexpert fingers of the youth of Rumbury Town.

Miss Lestrange walked fast, talking to herself, as elderly people do who lead solitary lives.

'If he were ill he might ask for me,' she muttered, going past Gay Injectors and Ejectors without sparing a thought to wonder what obscure goods or services their name denoted. 'He once said he might; I remember his saying that if he were taken ill he might get in touch with me; it's queer that I can hardly remember what we quarrelled about, and yet I can remember that.'

The alley took a turn, widened, and led her into a melancholy little area of street market: crockery stalls, cheap clothing stalls, vegetable stalls, second-hand book and junk stalls. The traders were just closing up for the night, piling their unsold wares – of which there seemed a great many – back into cartons; the way was impeded by boxes of rubbish, and slippery with squashed vegetables, but Miss Lestrange stepped briskly round and over these obstacles without appearing to notice them.

'What did we quarrel about, all that long time ago?' she mused, neatly by-passing a pram loaded with dusty tins of furniture polish and stepping over a crate labelled SUPERSHINE WHOLESALE: WE PROMISE DAZZLING RESULTS. 'It was something to do with his poetry, was it?'

The lane narrowed again and she went on between great overhanging cliffs of blackened brick, frowning a little, over her pince-nez, as she tried to summon up a young, lively, impatient face. What had he looked like, exactly? At one time she had known his face by heart – better than her own, for Miss Lestrange had never been one to spend much time gazing at herself in mirrors. Noticeable cheek-bones; a lock of hair that always fell forward; that was all she could remember.

We Promise Dazzling Results.

'I don't *know* anything about poetry, Tom. How can I say if it's good or bad?'

'You've got an *opinion*, haven't you, girl? You can say what you *think*?'

'You don't really want me to say what I think. You just want me to praise them.'

'Damn it, that's not true, January. January!' he said bitterly. 'There never was a more appropriate bit of classi-fication. If ever anybody was ice-cold, frozen hard, un-generous, utterly unwilling to give an inch, it's you!'

'*That*'s not true!' she had wanted to cry. 'It's just that I can't praise what I don't understand, I won't make pretty speeches just to encourage. How can I tell about your poetry? How can I say if I don't know? It wouldn't be right.'

But he had already stuffed the disputed poems into an

old black satchel and gone striding off; that was the last time she had seen him.

She passed a café with an inscription in what looked like white grease on its window-glass: Sausages, potatoes, onions, peas; frying now, always frying. Why not try our fry?

A staggeringly strong, hot waft of sausage and onion came from the open door; inside were boys with tiny heads, tiny eyes, and huge feet in huge boots; as she hurried by, Miss Lestrange felt their eyes investigating her and then deciding that she was not worth the trouble. The hot smell of food made her feel sick and reminded her that she was trembling with hunger; for her lunch at midday she had eaten half a hard-boiled egg, for her breakfast a cup of milkless tea.

'I suppose I shall have to put my fees up,' she thought, frowning again.

A shrill whistle, with something familiar about it, disturbed her train of thought, and she glanced ahead. It was the tune, not the whistle, that was familiar: in a moment she identified it as a tune she had written herself, an easy tune for beginners on the harp; she had called it *Snowdrops*.

And, rollerskating heedlessly in her direction, whistling it shrilly, but in tune, came the boy to whom she had just finished giving a lesson earlier that evening when Dr Smith arrived.

Their surprise at meeting was equal. He had almost run into her; he skidded to a jerky stop, braking himself with a hand on the alley wall.

'Miss Lestrange! Coo, *you*'re a long way from home, aren't you? You lost your way?'

'Good evening, David. No, I have not lost my way,' Miss Lestrange replied briskly. 'I am simply taking a walk.' What is there surprising in that? her tone expressed.

David looked startled; then he gave her a teasing, disbelieving grin, which made his crooked eyebrows shoot off round the corners of his face. She had never noticed this trick before; but then of course in his lessons he never *did* grin; he was always sweatingly anxious and subdued.

'*I* don't believe you're just out for a walk; I think you're after that there buried treasure!'

'Buried treasure? What buried treasure, pray?'

'Why, the treasure they say's buried somewhere under the middle o' Rumbury Town. That's what *you*'re after! But you won't find it! They say the old Devil's keeping an eye on it for himself. If I were you, Miss Lestrange, I'd turn back before you *do* get lost!'

'I shall do no such thing,' Miss Lestrange said firmly, and she went on her way, and David went skating zigzag on *his* way, whistling again the little tune, *Snowdrops* – 'Mi, re, doh, Snowdrops in the snow . . .'

But Miss Lestrange did turn and look once after David, slightly puzzled. He was so different, so much livelier and more sure of himself than during her lessons; he had quite surprised her.

But as for getting lost – what nonsense.

Nevertheless, in a couple of minutes, without being aware of it, Miss Lestrange did lose herself. She came to a point where five alleys met at an open space shaped like a star, chose one at random, walked a fair way along it, came to another similar intersection, and chose again. Rumbury Town folded itself round her. The green sky overhead was turning to navy-blue.

And all around her was dark, too; like the crater of an extinct volcano. An occasional orange streetlight dimly illuminated the alleyway. Not a sound was to be heard. It was a dead world.

Suddenly Miss Lestrange felt uneasy. Her thoughts flew to the professional visit taking place behind her, from the vision of which she had so determinedly started away. Jane must have left him by now. Probably in the car, wondering where I've got to. I had better turn back.

She turned back. And came to the first of the star-shaped conjunctions of lanes.

'Which was mine?' She stood wondering. All four openings facing her looked blank, like shut drawers; she could find no recognizable feature in any of them. The names were just visible: Lambskin Alley, New Year Way, Peridot Lane, Hell Passage; none of them did she consciously remember seeing before.

'I'd surely have noticed New Year Way,' she thought, and so chose Hell Passage – not that it looked any more familiar than the rest. What may have caught her unwitting ear was the faint thrum and throb of music, somewhere far away in that direction; as she proceeded along the narrow passage the sound became steadily more identifiable as music, though Miss Lestrange could not put a name to the actual *tune*; but then the world of pop music was unfamiliar territory to her. At least, though, music meant people, and inhabited regions; just for a minute or two, back there, although she would not have admitted it to anybody, Miss Lestrange had felt a stirring of panic at the vacuum of silence all round her.

On she went; crossed another star-shaped conjunction of alleys and, by the light of one high-up orange sodium tube, hung where the youth of Rumbury Town were unlikely to be able to break it by throwing bottles, saw that Hell Passage still continued, bisecting the angle between Sky Peals Lane and Whalebone Way.

'Curious names they have hereabouts; it must be a very old quarter. I shall look up the names on the map if – when I get home. *Did* I come this way?' Miss Lestrange asked herself; another surge of anxiety and alarm swept over her as she passed the closed premises of the Prong,

Thong, and Trident Company – surely she would have noticed *that* on the way along?

But the music was much louder now; at least, soon, she must encounter somebody whom she could ask.

Then, without any question, she knew that she was lost. For Hell Passage came to a stop – or rather, it opened into a little cul-de-sac yard out of which there was no other exit. Miss Lestrange could see quite plainly that there was no other exit because the yard was illuminated by a fierce, flickering, variable light which came from bundles of tarry rags stuffed into road-menders' tripods and burning vigorously. These were set against the walls. There were about a dozen people in the yard, and Miss Lestrange's first reaction was one of relief.

'It's one of those pop groups,' she thought. 'I've heard it's hard for them, when they're starting, to find places to practise; I suppose if you can't afford to hire a studio, somewhere like this, far off and out of earshot, would be a godsend.'

Somehow the phrase *out of earshot*, though she had used it herself, made her feel uncomfortable; the beat and howl of the music, failing to fight its way out of the narrow court, was so tremendous, that it gave her a slight chill to think what a long way she must be from any residential streets, for people not to have complained about it.

She glanced again at the group; decided not to ask them her way, and turned to go quickly and quietly back. But she was too late; she found somebody standing behind her: an enormously large, tall man, dressed in red velvet trousers and jacket, with a frilled shirt.

'Hey, now, you're not thinking of *leaving*, are you – when you just got here?' His voice was a genial roar, easily heard even above the boom of the music, but there was a jeering note under its geniality. 'Surely not going to run off without hearing us, were you? Look, boys and girls,' he went on, his voice becoming, without the slightest difficulty, even louder, 'Look who's here! It's Miss Lestrange, Miss January Lestrange, come to give us her critical opinion!'

A wild shout of derisive laughter went up from the group in the court.

'Three cheers for Miss January Lestrange – the hippest harpist in the whole of toe-tapping Rumbury Town!'

They cheered her, on and on, and the tall man led her with grinning mock civility to a seat on an upturned Snowcem tin. The players began tuning their instruments, some of which, trumpets and basses, seemed conventional enough, but others were contrivances that Miss Lestrange had never laid eyes on before – zinc washtubs with strings stretched across, large twisted shells, stringed instruments that looked more like weapons – crossbows, perhaps – than zithers, strange prehistoric-looking wooden pipes at least six or seven feet long – and surely that was an actual *fire* burning under the kettle-drum?

'January!' the large man boomed, standing just behind the shoulder of Miss Lestrange. 'Now, *there*'s a chilly sort of name to give a spirited lady like yourself – a downright cold, miserable kind of a dreary name, isn't it, boys and girls? The worst month of the year!'

'It is not!' snapped Miss Lestrange – but she did wish he would not stand so close, for his presence just out of sight gave her the cold grue – for some odd reason the phrase *Get thee behind me, Satan*, slipped into her mind – 'January means hope, it means looking forward, because the whole year lies ahead.'

But her retort was drowned in the shout from the group of players – '*We*'ll soon warm her up!'

'Happy lot, ain't they?' confided the voice at her back. 'Nick's Nightflowers, we call ourselves – from the location, see?' He pointed up and, by the light of the flaring

rags, Miss Lestrange could just read the sign on the wall:
OLD NICK'S COURT, E.I. 'And I'm Old Nick, naturally –
happy to have you with us tonight, Miss Lestrange.'

She flicked a glance sideways, to see if it would be
possible to slip away once they began playing, but to her
dismay most of the group were now between her and the
entrance, blocking the way; from their grins, it was plain
that they knew what she had in mind. And she had never
seen such an unattractive crew – 'Really,' she thought, 'if
they had *tails* they could hardly look less human.'

Old Nick, with his red velvet and ruffles, was about the
most normal in appearance and dress, but she cared for
him least of all, and unobtrusively edged her Snowcem
tin cornerways until at least she had the wall at her back.

'Ready, all? Cool it now – real cool,' called Nick, at
which there was a howl of laughter. 'One, two, three –
stomp!'

The music broke out again. If music it could be called.
The sound seemed to push Miss Lestrange's blood back-
ward along her arteries, to flog on her eardrums, to slam
in her lungs, to seize hold of her heart and dash it from
side to side.

'I shan't be able to endure it for more than a minute or
two,' she thought quite calmly. 'It's devilish, that's what
it is – really devilish.'

Just at the point when she had decided she could stand
it no longer, half a dozen more figures lounged forward
from a shadow at the side of the court, and began to dance.
Boys or girls? It was hard to say. They seemed bald, and
extraordinarily *thin* – they had white, hollow faces, deep-
set eyes under bulging foreheads, meaningless grins.
'White satin!' thought Miss Lestrange scornfully. 'And
ruffles! What an extraordinarily dated kind of costume –
like the pierrot troupes when I was young.'

But at closer view the satin seemed transparent gauze,

or chiffon. 'I've never *seen* anyone so thin – they are like something out of Belsen,' thought Miss Lestrange. 'That one must have had rickets when young – his legs are no more than bones. They must all have had rickets,' she decided.

'D'you like it?' boomed the leader in her ear. It seemed amazing that he could still make his voice heard above the row, but he could.

'Frankly, no,' said Miss Lestrange. 'I never laid eyes on such a spiritless ensemble. They all dance as if they wanted dosing with Parrish's Food and codliver oil.'

'Hear that, gang?' he bawled to the troupe. 'Hear that? The lady doesn't care for your dancing; she thinks you're a lily-livered lot.'

The dancers paused; they turned their bloodless faces towards Miss Lestrange. For a moment she quailed, as tiny lights seemed to burn in the deep eye-sockets, all fixed on her. But then the leader shouted,

'And what's more, *I* think so too! Do it again – and this time, put some guts into it, or it'll be prong, thong, and trident, all right!'

The players redoubled their pace and volume, the dancers broke into a faster shuffle. And the leader, still making himself heard above the maniac noise, shouted,

'Hope! Where are you? Come along out, you mangy old tom-cat, you!' And, to the group, '*He*'ll soon tickle you up!'

A dismal and terrified wailing issued from the dancers at these words.

'Hope's a little pet of mine,' confided the leader to Miss Lestrange. 'Makes all the difference when they're a bit sluggish; *you* ought to like him too.'

She distrusted his tone, which seemed to promise some highly unpleasant surprise, and looked round sharply.

A kind of ripple parted the musicians and dancers; at

first Miss Lestrange could not see what had caused this, but, even through the music, she thought she could hear cries of pain or terror; then a wave of dancers eddied away from her and a gold-brown animal bounded through, snatching with sabre-teeth at a bony thigh as it passed.

'That's Hope,' said the leader with satisfaction. '*That*'s my little tiger-kitten. Isn't he a beauty? Isn't he a ducky-diddums? I powder his fur with pepper and ginger before we start, to put him in a lively mood – and *then* doesn't he chase them about if they're a bit mopish!'

Hope certainly had a galvanizing effect upon the dancers; as he slunk and bounded among them, their leaps and gyrations had the frenzy of a tarantella; sometimes he turned and made a sudden snarling foray among the musicians, which produced a wild flurry of extra discords and double drumbeats.

'Here, puss, puss! Nice pussy, then! There's a lady here who'd like to stroke you.'

Hope turned, and silently sprang in their direction. Miss Lestrange had her first good look at him. He was bigger than a leopard, a brownish-ginger colour all over, with long, angrily switching tail; his fangs glistened white-gold in the fiery light, his eyes blazed like carbuncles; he came towards Miss Lestrange slowly, stalking, with head lowered.

And she put out her right hand, confidently running it over his shoulder-blades and along the curving, knobbed spine; its bristles undulated under the light pressure. 'There, then!' she said absently. Hope turned, and rubbed his harsh ruff against her hand; elevated his chin to be scratched; finally sat down beside her and swung the long tail neatly into place over formidable talons.

Miss Lestrange thoughtfully pulled his ears; she had always liked cats.

She turned to the leader again.

'I still don't think much of your dancers. And, to be honest, your music seems to me nothing but a diabolical row!'

Silence followed her words. She felt the dark cavities in their faces trained on her, and forced herself not to shrink.

'However, thank you for playing to me. And now I must be going,' she ended politely.

'Dear me.' The leader's tone was thoughtful. 'That fairly puts us in our place, don't it, boys and girls? You certainly are a free-spoken one, Miss January Lestrange. Come now – I'm sure a nice lady, a dyed-in-the-wool lady like you, wouldn't want to be too hard on the lads, and *really* upset them. Just before you go – if you *do* go – tell me, don't you think that, in time, if they practise hard enough, they might amount to something?'

'I am absolutely not prepared to make such a statement,' Miss Lestrange said firmly. 'Your kind of music is quite outside my province. And I have never believed in flattery.' A kind of rustle ran through the group; they moved closer.

'Our kind of music ain't her province,' the leader said. 'That's true. Tell you what, Miss Lestrange. *You* shall give *us* a tune. Let's have some of *your* kind of music – eh? That'd be a treat for us, wouldn't it, gang?'

They guffawed, crowding closer and closer; she bit her lip.

'Fetch over the harp!' bawled Nick. 'No one in our ensemble actually plays it,' he explained to Miss Lestrange. 'But we like to have one along always – you never know when someone may turn up who's a harp fancier. Like you. No strings, I'm afraid, but we can fix that, easy.'

A warped, battered, peeling old harp was dumped down before her; it had no strings, but one of the dancers dragged up a coil of what looked like telephone cable and began rapidly stringing it to and fro across the frame.

'Now,' said Nick, 'you shall delight us, Miss Lestrange! And if you *do*, then maybe we'll see about allowing you to leave. Really, you know, we'd hate to part from you.'

An expectant silence had fallen: an unpleasant, mocking, triumphant silence.

'I haven't the least intention of playing that ridiculous instrument,' Miss Lestrange said coldly. 'And now, I'm afraid you'll have to excuse me; my friend will be wondering where I've got to. Come, Hope.'

She turned and walked briskly to the entrance of the court; there was no need to push her way, they parted before her. Hope trotted at her side.

Far off, down Hell Passage, could be heard a faint, clear whistle, coming her way.

But, once out in the alley, Miss Lestrange tottered, and nearly fell; she was obliged to put a hand against the wall to support herself. Seized with a deep chill and trembling, she was afraid to trust her unsteady legs, and had to wait until the boy David reached her, whistling and zig-zagging along on his rollerskates.

'Coo, Miss Lestrange, I *knew* you'd get lost; and you did, didn't you? Thought I'd better come back and see where you'd got to. You all right?' he said, sharply scrutinizing her face.

'Yes, thank you, David. I'm quite all right now. I just went a bit farther than I intended. I'm a little tired, that's all.'

She glanced back into Old Nick's Court. It was empty: empty and silent. The flares had gone out.

'Well, come on then, Miss Lestrange, just you follow me and I'll take you back to the other lady's car. You can hold on to my anorak if you like,' he suggested.

'That's all right, thank you David, I can manage now.'

So he skated slowly ahead and she walked after him,

and a little way in the rear Hope followed, trotting silently in the shadows.

When they came within view of the car – it took a very short time, really – David said, 'I'll say good night then, Miss Lestrange. See you Thursday.'

'Good night, David, and thank you.' Then she called after him: 'Practise hard, now!'

'Okay, Miss Lestrange.'

There was an ambulance drawn up behind the car.

'Wait there!' she said to Hope. He sat down in the shadows of the alley-mouth.

As Miss Lestrange crossed the road, the ambulance rolled off. Dr Smith stood looking after it.

'Sorry to be such a time,' she said. 'That poor man – I'm afraid he's not going to make it.'

'You mean – Tom Rampisham?'

'I shouldn't be surprised if he dies on the way in. Oh – excuse me a moment – I'll have to lock up his flat and give the key to the porter.'

Without thinking about it, Miss Lestrange followed her ex-pupil. She walked into the untidy room that she had last entered – how long? thirty years ago? – and looked at the table, covered with scrawled sheets of paper.

'I don't know who ought to take charge of this,' Dr Smith said, frowning. 'I suppose he has a next-of-kin somewhere. Well – I'll worry about that tomorrow. Come along – *you* must be starving and exhausted – let's go.'

Miss Lestrange was looking at the top sheet, at the heading HOPE, which was printed in large capitals. Half-way down the page a sentence began.

'*It was on a clear, frosty November evening, not many years ago . . .*'

The words tailed off into a blob of ink.

Dr Smith led the way out. 'It's terribly late. We can still get a meal at the Chinese place, though,' she was saying. 'And afterwards I'll phone up Rumbury Central and find out how – and find out. I really am sorry to have kept you so long. I hope you weren't frozen and bored.'

'No . . . No. I – I went for a walk.'

Miss Lestrange followed the doctor along the echoing concrete passage. And as she went – 'I do hope,' she was thinking, 'oh, I do *hope* that Hope will still be there.'

The Lost Five Minutes

THERE was once a dragon who kept a museum and did quite well from it. He had become (at some point during the several thousand years of his life) rather bored with just eating people, and the museum made a nice change and a new interest. He charged ten pence entry fee and instead of requests to the public not to smoke and climb over the guard ropes and touch the exhibits, there were simply signs saying, 'If you do not behave yourself properly the dragon will eat you.'

You'd think such signs might have stopped people from being very keen to visit the museum. Not a bit of it; there was a kind of daredevil fascination about going there. People simply flocked. Maybe it was from the excitement of not knowing quite what the dragon would consider proper behaviour, maybe – human nature being what it is – because everyone had a sneaking hope of seeing somebody else misbehave and get swallowed. But quite apart from these reasons, the museum was a particularly nice and unusual one, everything in it being made of glass. In the main hall stood Cinderella's glass coach and slippers, on the first floor was a glass doll's house all complete with furniture, lovely music was played all day long on a glass harmonica, and in smaller rooms there were collections of glass fruit from Venice (every colour of the rainbow), glass animals, and a whole aviary full of birds with spun-glass tails.

For that matter the dragon himself was made of glass: stretched out in the sun or coiled round the great ilex tree in front of his museum he made a stunning spectacle, each feather and scale flashing like a frozen waterfall, his three heads keeping a sharp lookout for customers in every direction. It was due to his three heads, in fact, that the dragon had given up his regular habit of eating people, since, either because of old age or greed or just general cantankerousness, the heads could never come to an agreement over whose turn it was to swallow the next victim. And all this fuss before meals gave the dragon indigestion and hiccups, so, on the whole, he had found it simpler not to swallow anybody. Of course the public did not know this.

In every museum there has to be somebody to dust the exhibits and take the entry money, unlock the doors in the morning, and tell people where to find the ladies' room. The dragon had occasionally encountered difficulty in hiring assistants, but at present he was very well suited: the post was filled by a blind girl called Anthea, who was extremely careful and conscientious, besides being very pretty; she never broke anything when she dusted, having that extra sixth radar-sense of where objects are that blind people often possess; she wasn't a bit frightened of the dragon, since she had never seen how huge and dazzling he was; and because she was blind, people never tried to cheat her out of the ten-pence entry fees. And in the evenings she told fairy tales to the dragon, which also made a pleasant change for him. Nobody had ever done such a thing before.

One day, however, Anthea came to grief.

The dragon had recently come by a new treasure for his museum: a very beautiful clock, every single part made of glass, hands, face, chimes, pendulum, mainspring, and all. It stood under a glass dome and when you looked at it you felt that you could see time itself in motion. The clock was more than five hundred years old and had neither lost nor gained a minute, nor stopped, since the day it was first wound up.

Well! Anthea had been showing the clock to the editor of the local paper, the *Wormley Observer*. He was a fat little fellow, all smiles, called Sam Inkfellow. She was just replacing the glass dome when somebody jogged her elbow. Instinctively Anthea clasped both hands round the dome to steady it, and set it carefully down, but as she did so she tipped it – *very* slightly – against the works of the clock, shaking loose five minutes from the mainspring. And before she could push the dome straight, the five minutes had slipped out from underneath and darted away through the museum window, like a handful of bees escaped from the hive.

The museum had a very efficient alarm system. Bells began to clang, doors automatically slammed, two carloads of police came whizzing round from headquarters, and the dragon cascaded off his ilex tree like a glacier from an erupting volcano. But the mischief was done: the five minutes could not be recovered.

'It was my fault,' poor Anthea said to the police. 'Please let everyone go, nobody has stolen anything. It was entirely my fault.'

The police could only agree. All the members of the public who had been shut in by the automatic doors were allowed to go.

'You realize this means I shall have to swallow you?' the dragon said very crossly to Anthea.

'Yes I know; I really am sorry; please go ahead and get it over with.'

'Certainly not; things must be done in due order,' the dragon said hurriedly. 'I shall swallow you a week today, next Thursday, at eight a.m.' For he was not at all pleased at the troublesome prospect of having to find a new assistant, nor at the likelihood of hiccups and indigestion. 'After all, somebody may return the five minutes before then.'

He stuck up a sign saying LOST: FIVE MINUTES. FINDER PLEASE RETURN TO WORMLEY MUSEUM. REWARD.

Meantime the *Wormley Observer* came out with huge headlines: DRAGON TO SWALLOW ANTHEA NEXT THURSDAY A.M.

Special excursion buses were to be run to the town from as far away as Brighton, the *Observer* published a timetable of events, and wooden seats were hastily erected in the main square facing the museum. Extra police were fetched in and a one-way traffic system organized; the shops sold little dragon flags, a commemorative stamp was issued, and a public holiday was proclaimed.

'All this publicity is very distasteful,' said the dragon.

'I really am sorry,' said Anthea.

But Sam Inkfellow, editor of the *Wormley Observer*, was rubbing his hands. He had a guaranteed sale of eighty thousand copies for next week's issue (in full colour), the Press Association had paid him large sums for the story with pictures, and he was charging ten guineas a head standing room in the *Observer* offices, which overlooked the square.

Anthea's family were very upset. Her brother Bill came and tried to reason with the dragon.

'Can't you substitute some other penalty?' he asked.

'Sorry,' said the dragon. 'I regret the necessity quite as much as you. But rules are rules. You produce the lost five minutes, I'll cancel the swallowing.'

'Would any five minutes do?'

'Oh, certainly, just so long as they are a *spare* five minutes.'

When he heard this, Bill became slightly more cheerful. Surely, he thought, someone about the town must have five minutes to spare. Or even three, or two; it shouldn't be impossible to collect a few minutes together.

Elderly people seemed likelier to have time to spare, so he called on the old lady who lived next door to his mother. She was working in her garden, picking up scattered rose petals and brushing all the grass blades straight, so that they pointed in one direction.

'Mrs Pentecost, could you possibly spare five minutes for my sister Anthea? Or even two, or one?'

'Oh, good gracious, no, my dear boy! Why, when you get to my age, there's so little time left that you have to hoard every minute like gold. Sorry, but no, no indeed!'

Perhaps it would be better to try somebody young, Bill thought, so he went to a schoolmate of Anthea's.

'Sally, could you possibly spare me a minute or two for Anthea?'

'Oh, honestly, Bill darling, I'm so rushed I haven't a *second* to spare, let alone a minute, what with getting my hairpiece set, and my false lashes stuck on, and my nail varnish dried, and reading my horoscope in *Seventeen*, and looking for a new leather jacket –'

Bill saw that he would get no help there.

Nobody, anywhere, had any time to spare, not just at that moment.

'If you were to come back next week –' they said. 'Now next week I'll have *plenty* of spare time. Or next month, even better. But just *now*, I do seem to be so terribly short of time –'

So it went on, all week. On Wednesday evening Bill went to see the dragon.

'Can't you suggest anybody, sir?'

The dragon scratched one of his glass chins, with a sound like icicles tinkling together.

'What about the town genius?' he suggested after a while.

'That's a good idea!' said Bill. 'Why didn't I think of it? I'll go directly.'

And he got on his bicycle and set out.

The town genius, whose name was Marcantonio Smith-to-the-power-Nine, did not live in the town nowadays; he had done so, but found he got little work done because people constantly came to him asking him to solve their problems. So now he lived in a tower with a studio in the nearby forest, where he painted, and sculpted, and wrote poetry, and conceived new kinds of mathematics, and invented perpetual motion, and did everything a genius ought.

Bill found him in the studio, standing in front of a huge slab of marble. On the marble he had a football-sized lump of colourless, shining material, like nothing so much in the world as a good big bit of glass putty, and he was squeezing it, and kneading it, and thumping it, and palming it into a ball, and then flattening it out, and then rolling it into a sausage, and then tearing it into thin strips, and those into small nuggets, shaping them all into different things, animals, stars, flowers, figures, faces, and then flinging the whole mass together and beginning again.

He smiled kindly at Bill, who came hesitating over and stood by the slab.

'Well, my boy? What can I do for you?'

All this time Smith never stopped playing with his lump of stuff.

Bill told the sad tale of Anthea and the lost five minutes.

'I was wondering if you could possibly help us,' he said. 'The dragon's due to swallow her tomorrow at eight sharp unless I can find somebody to give me five minutes.'

'Five minutes? Is that all?' said Marcantonio Smith-to-the-power-Nine, and he pinched off a bit of his glass putty. 'Do you want them marked out?' He flattened the small lump he had pinched off, shaped it into an oblong, and marked five divisions on it as if he were scoring fudge.

Bill gaped, watching him, and he laughed.

'No need to look so astonished, my boy!'

'It seems so easy for you!'

'It's always easy to be kind.'

'It didn't seem so for the other people in the town,' Bill said. 'How is it you have so much time when nobody else has any at all?'

'That's because I only do the things that interest me. Do you want your five minutes in a bag?'

'Oh, please don't trouble, sir. I wish I could do something for you!'

'Bring your sister to visit me sometime. I like fairy tales too.'

Bill promised he would, and hurried off with his precious little slab of minutes.

But on the way home he met a man mending a puncture in his motor bike tyre.

'Oh, my dear boy! Is that five minutes you have there? Do, do give me just a couple of them – *please*! I'm on my way with a pardon for my son, who is to be shot for a crime he didn't commit, and I got this puncture – I shall be too late – do, please help me!'

Bill was very upset. I can't let the poor man's son be shot for a crime he didn't commit, though, he thought; maybe the dragon will let me off two of the minutes.

Very carefully he broke two off his little cake of five.

'Heaven bless you, my boy. You're a real friend in need!'

Bill went on his way. Near the town harbour he met a man running downhill, hell-for-leather.

'Help!' he called. 'Is that three minutes you've got there? Give me two of them, like a good lad! Do you see that ship, that's just casting off anchor? If only I can get to her before she sails, I've got a bit of paper to deliver on board that will stop two great countries going to war against each other, but I'm going to be too late – for heaven's sake help me!'

Very unwillingly, Bill gave him a couple of minutes – maybe, after all, the dragon will be satisfied with just one, he thought – and the man rushed away down the hill.

Now there was only one minute left. And as Bill was passing the school, a teacher put his head out of the window and said,

'Please, my dear boy! I see that is a spare minute you have in your hand. Be a good lad and give it here – if I had just *one* minute more, before the end-of-period bell went, I could teach this class of thickheads how to save the world!'

Well, you can't refuse a request like that, can you? So Bill handed over his last minute. By now it was seven o'clock Thursday morning.

So Bill went along to the dragon and explained that, although Mr Smith had given him five minutes, due to one reason or another he had been obliged to part with them.

'Since it's now my fault the five minutes are lost,' he said, 'will you please swallow me instead of Anthea?'

The dragon considered. He saw the benefits of this arrangement, because at least Anthea would then still be available to dust the exhibits and tell him fairy tales at night.

'Very well,' he said at length grudgingly. 'But you are both putting me to a lot of trouble.'

By now huge crowds of people were gathered in Wormley Square, all anxious to watch the swallowing.

'Ma,' said a child to his mother, 'shall we be able to see the young lady go all the way down inside the dragon?'

'D'you think he'll chew her?' said a man to his wife.

'I am excited, Henry!' said a girl to her boyfriend. 'Which head will he swallow with, d'you think?'

This remark was overheard by the dragon's heads, who instantly began arguing.

'Belial had the last swallow, it's my turn!'

'No it isn't, Thammuz, it's mine!'

'Shut up, Dagon and Belial, it's neither of you, it's my turn!'

The dragon retired behind his ilex to sort the matter out. Eight o'clock struck and people began to grumble because nothing had happened.

'What's the crowd waiting for?' asked a traveller in false teeth who happened to be passing through the town.

'Don't you know? Our dragon's going to swallow the young lady because she let five minutes escape from the clock last Thursday.'

'No, she didn't, it was five hours!'

'Anyway it isn't her, it's the young gentleman he's going to swallow.'

'It wasn't from the clock they escaped.'

'They didn't escape, he ran over them on his motor bike and squashed them flat.'

'No he didn't, they rolled down the hill and fell on to a ship!'

'That's a lie! My hubby told me the teacher at the school gave them to his physics class and they dissolved them in sulphuric acid!'

Everybody began arguing. People came to blows.

But the traveller pushed his way to the ilex tree and said to the dragon,

'If you are really about to swallow that young lady for losing five minutes, you are being unfair! I happened to be in your museum last Thursday and I saw that man there jog her elbow. He did it on purpose. *He*'s the one you ought to swallow!'

'Really?' said the dragon, and he turned to the man the traveller had indicated and swallowed him down without more ado (Belial happened to be the nearest head and did the job). Everybody saw fat little Sam Inkfellow travel slowly and spirally down through all the glass coils. It took a long time, gave the dragon frightful indigestion and hiccups, and he was sorry for himself for three days after, but all the townspeople were delighted, as Inkfellow had published unpleasant, and mostly untrue, stories about them all in his paper at one time or another.

'No hard feelings, I hope?' said the dragon to Anthea when his hiccups had died down and he was feeling better. 'You'll come back and start helping in the museum again, won't you?'

'I'm afraid not,' said Anthea. 'No hard feelings, but Bill and I are going to go and work for the town genius. So goodbye.'

And that is what they did. The dragon had terrible trouble finding another assistant. And in the end, Anthea married Marcantonio Smith-to-the-power-Nine.

The Rose of Puddle Fratrum

RIGHT, then: imagine this little village, not far back from the sea, in the chalk country, Puddle Fratrum is its name. One dusty, narrow street, winding along from the Haymakers' Arms to Mrs Sherborne's Bed and Breakfast (with french marigolds and bachelors' buttons in the front garden): halfway between these two, at an acute bend, an old old grey stone house, right on the pavement, but with a garden behind hidden from the prying eyes of strangers by a ten-foot wall. And the house itself – now here's a queer thing – the house itself covered all over *thick*, doors, windows, and all, by a great climbing rose, fingering its way up to the gutters and over the stone-slabbed roof, sending out tendrils this way and that, round corners, over sills, through crevices, till the place looks not so much like a house, more like a mound of vegetation, a great green thorny thicket.

In front of it, a B.B.C. man, standing and scratching his head.

Presently the B.B.C. man, whose name was Rodney Cushing, walked along to the next building, which was a forge.

TOBIAS PROUT, BLACKSMITH AND FARRIER, said the sign, and there he was, white-haired, leather-aproned, with a pony's bent knee gripped under his elbow, trying on a red-hot shoe for size.

Rodney waited until the fizzling and sizzling and smell of burnt coconut had died down, and then he asked,

'Can you tell me if that was the ballerina's house?' – pointing at the rose-covered clump.

B.B.C. men are used to anything, but Rodney was a bit

startled when the blacksmith, never even answering, hurled the red-hot pony shoe at the stone wall of his forge (where it buckled into a figure-eight and sizzled some more), turned his back, and stomped to an inner room where he began angrily working his bellows and blowing up his forge fire.

Rodney, seeing no good was to be had from the black-smith, walked along to the Haymakers' Arms.

'Can you tell me,' he said to Mr Donn the landlord over a pint of old and mild, 'can you tell me anything about the house with the rose growing over it?'

'Arr,' said the landlord.

'Did it belong to a ballet dancer?'

'Maybe so.'

'Famous thirty years back?'

'Arr.'

'By name Rose Collard?'

'Arr,' said the landlord. 'The Rose of Puddle Fratrum, they did use to call her. And known as far afield as Axminster and Poole.'

'She was known all over the world.'

'That may be. I can only speak for these parts.'

'I'm trying to make a film about her life, for the B.B.C. I daresay plenty of people in the village remember her?'

'Arr. Maybe.'

'I was asking the blacksmith, but he didn't answer.'

'Deaf. Deaf as an adder.'

'He didn't seem deaf,' Rodney said doubtfully.

'None so deaf as them what won't hear. All he hears is nightingales.'

'Oh. How very curious. Which reminds me, can you put me up for the night?'

'Not I,' said the landlord gladly. 'Old Mrs Sherborne's fule enough for that, though; she'll have ye.'

Mrs Sherborne, wrinkled and tart as a dried apricot,

was slightly more prepared to be communicative about
the Rose of Puddle Fratrum.

'My second cousin by marriage, poor thing,' she said,
clapping down a plate with a meagre slice of Spam, two
lettuce leaves, and half a tomato. 'Slipped on a banana-
peel, she did ('twas said one of the scene-shifters dropped
it on the stage); mortification set in, they had to take her
leg off, that was the end of her career.'

'Did she die? Did she retire? What happened to
her?'

In his excitement and interest, Rodney swallowed Spam,
lettuce, tomato, and all, at one gulp. Mrs Sherborne
pressed her lips together and carried away his plate.

'Came back home, went into a decline, never smiled
again,' she said, returning with two prunes and half a
dollop of junket so thickly powdered over with nutmeg
that it looked like sandstone. 'Let the rose grow all over
the front of her house, wouldn't answer the door,
wouldn't see a soul. Some say she died. Some say she went
abroad. Some say she's still there and the nightingales
fetch her food. (Wonderful lot of nightingales we do have
hereabouts, all the year round.) But one thing they're all
agreed on.'

'What's that?' The prunes and junket had gone the
way of the Spam in one mouthful; shaking her head, Mrs
Sherborne replaced them with two dry biscuits and a
square centimetre of processed cheese wrapped in a seam-
less piece of foil that defied all attempts to discover its
opening.

'When she hurt her leg she was a-dancing in a ballet
that was writ for her special. About a rose and a nightingale, it was. They say that for one scene they had to have
the stage knee-deep in rose-petals – fresh every night, too!
Dear dear! Think of the cost?'

Mrs Sherborne looked sadly at the mangled remains of

the cheese (Rodney had managed to haggle his way
through the foil somehow) and carried it away.

'Well, and so?' Rodney asked, when she came back
into the dark, damp little parlour with a small cup of
warm water into which a minute quantity of Dark Tan
shoe-polish had almost certainly been dissolved. 'What
about this ballet?'

''Twas under all the rose-petals the banana-peel had
been dropped. That was how she came to slip on it. So
when Rose Collard retired she laid a curse on the ballet –
she came of a witch family, there's always been a-plenty
witches in these parts, as well as nightingales,' Mrs
Sherborne said, nodding dourly, and Rodney thought she
might easily qualify for membership of the Puddle
Fratrum and District Witches' Institute herself – 'laid a
curse on the ballet. "Let no company ever put it on
again," says she, a-sitting in her wheelchair, "or, sure as I
sit here –"'

'Sure as I sit here, what?' asked Rodney eagerly.

'I disremember exactly. The dancer as took Rose's part
would break *her* leg, or the stage'd collapse, or there'd be
some other desprat mischance. Anyway, from that day to
this, no one's ever dared to do that ballet, not nowhere
in the world.'

Rodney nodded gloomily. He already knew this. It had
been extremely difficult even to get hold of a copy of the
score and choreographic script. *The Nightingale and the Rose*
had been based on a version of a story by Oscar Wilde.
Music had been specially written by Augustus Irish,
choreography by Danny Pashkinski, costumes and
scenery designed by Rory el Moro. The original costumes
were still laid away in mothballs in the Royal Museum of
Ballet. Rodney was having nylon copies made for his film.

'Well, you won't be wanting nothing *more*, I don't
suppose,' Mrs Sherborne said, as if Rod might be expected

to demand steak tartare and praline ice. 'Here's the bath plug, I daresay you will wish to retire as the TV's out of order. Put the plug back in the kitchen after you've had your bath.'

This was presumably to discourage Rodney from the sin of taking two baths in quick succession, but he had no wish to do so. The water was hardly warmer than the coffee. When he ran it into the tiny bath, a sideways trickle from the base of the tap flowed on to the floor, alarming an enormous spider so much that all the time Rodney was in the bath he could hear it scurrying agitatedly about the linoleum. A notice beside a huge canister of scouring powder said PLEASE LEAVE THIS BATH CLEAN, after which some guest with spirit still unbroken had added WHY USE IT OTHERWISE?

Shivering, Rodney dropped the bath plug in the kitchen sink and went to his room. But the bed had only one thin, damp blanket; he got dressed again, and leaned out of the window. Some nightingales were beginning to tune up in the distance. The summer night was cool and misty, with a great vague moon sailing over the dim silvered roofs of Puddle Fratrum. Due to the extreme curve in the village street, the corner of Mrs Sherborne's back garden touched on another, enclosed by a high wall, which Rod was almost sure was that of the legendary Rose Collard.

He began to ponder. He scratched his head.

Then, going to his suitcase, he extracted a smallish piece of machinery, unfolded it, and set it up. It stood on one leg, with a tripod foot.

Rodney pulled out a kind of drawer on one side of this gadget, revealing a bank of lettered keys. On these he typed the message,

'Hullo, Fred.'

The machine clicked, rumbled, let out one or two long experimental rasping chirrs, not at all unlike the nightingales warming up, and then replied in a loud creaking voice,

'Friday evening June twelve nineteen seventy eight thirty p.m. Good evening, Rodney.'

The door shot open. Mrs Sherborne came boiling in.

'What's this?' she cried indignantly. 'I let the room to *one*, no more. Entertaining visitors in bedrooms is strictly against the –' She stopped, her mouth open. 'What's *that*?'

'My travelling computer,' Rodney replied.

Mrs Sherborne gave the computer a long, doubtful, suspicious glare. But at last she retired, saying, 'Well, all right. But if there's any noise, or bangs, mind, or if neighbours complain, you'll have to leave, immediate!'

'I have problems, Fred,' Rodney typed rapidly as soon as the door closed. 'Data up to the present about Rose Collard are as follows': and he added a summary of all that he had learned, adding, 'People in the village are unhelpful. What do you advise?'

Fred brooded, digesting the information that had been fed in.

'You should climb over the garden wall,' he said at length.

'I was afraid you'd suggest that,' Rodney typed resignedly. Then he closed Fred's drawer and folded his leg, took a length of rope from a small canvas holdall, and went downstairs. Mrs Sherborne poked her head out of the kitchen when she heard Rodney open the front door.

'I lock up at ten sharp,' she snapped.

'I hope you have fun,' Rodney said amiably, and went out.

He walked a short way, found a narrow alley to his left, and turned down it, finding, as he had hoped, that it circled round behind the walled garden of the rose-covered house. The wall, too, was covered by a climbing rose, very prickly, and although there was a door at the back it was locked, and plainly had not been opened for many years.

Rodney tossed up one end of his rope, which had a grappling-hook attached, and flicked it about until it gripped fast among the gnarled knuckles of the roses.

Inside the wall half a dozen nightingales were singing at the tops of their voices.

'The place sounds like a clock factory,' Rodney thought, pulling himself up and getting badly scratched. Squatting on top of the wall, he noticed that all the nightingales had fallen silent. He presumed that they were staring at him but he could not see them; the garden was full of rose-bushes run riot into twenty-foot clumps; no doubt the nightingales were sitting in these. But between the rose thickets were stretches of silvery grass; first freeing and winding up his rope, Rodney jumped down and began to wander quietly about. The nightingales started tuning up once more.

Rodney had not gone very far when something tapped him on the shoulder.

He almost fell over, so quickly did he spin round.

He had heard nothing, but there was a person behind him, sitting in a wheel-chair. Uncommon sight she was, to be sure, the whole of her bundled up in a shawl, with a great bush of moon-silvered white hair (he could see the drops of mist on it) and a long thin black stick (which was what she had tapped him with), ash-white face, thinner than the prow of a Viking ship, and a pair of eyes as dark as holes, steadily regarding him.

'And what do *you* want?' she said coldly.

'I – I'm sorry miss – ma'am,' Rodney stammered. 'I did knock, but nobody answered the door. Are you – could you be – Miss Rose Collard?'

'If I am,' said she, 'I don't see *that's* a cause for any

ex-Boy Scout with a rope and an extra share of impertinence to come climbing into my garden.'

'I'm from the B.B.C. I – we did write – care of Covent Garden. The letter was returned.'

'Well? I never answer letters. Now you *are* here, what do you want?'

'We are making a film about your life. Childhood in Puddle Fratrum. Career. And scenes from the ballet that was written for you.'

'So?'

'Well, Miss Collard, it's this curse you laid on it. I –' He hesitated, jabbed his foot into a dew-sodden silvery tussock of grass, and at last said persuasively, 'I don't suppose you could see your way to take the curse *off* again?'

'Why?' she asked with interest. 'Is it working?'

'*Working*! We've had one electricians' strike, two musicians', three studio fires, two cameras exploded, five dancers sprained their ankles. It's getting to be almost impossible to find anyone to take the part now.'

'My part? Who have you got at present?'

'A young dancer called Tessa Porutska. She's pretty inexperienced but – well, no one else would volunteer.'

Rose Collard smiled.

'So – well – couldn't you take the curse off? It's such a long time since it all happened.'

'Why should I take it off? What do I care about your studio fires or your sprained ankles?'

'If I brought Tess to see you? She's so keen to dance the part.'

'So was I keen once,' Rose Collard said, and she quoted dreamily, '"One red rose is all I want," cried the Nightingale.'

'It's such a beautiful ballet,' pleaded Rodney, 'or at least it *would* be, if only the stage didn't keep collapsing, and the props going astray, and the clarinettist getting hiccups –'

'Really? Did all those things happen? I never thought it would work half so well,' Rose Collard said wistfully, as if she rather hoped he would ask her to a rehearsal.

'What exactly were the terms of the curse?'

'Oh, just that some doom or misfortune should prevent the ballet ever being performed right through till Puddle church clock ran backwards, and the man who dropped the banana-peel said he was sorry, and somebody put on the ballet with a company of one-legged dancers.'

Rodney, who had looked moderately hopeful at the beginning of this sentence, let out a yelp of despair.

'We could probably fix the church clock. And surely we could get the chap to say he was sorry – where is he now, by the way?'

'How should I know?'

'But *one-legged* dancers! Have a heart, Miss Collard!'

'*I've* only got one leg!' she snapped. 'And I get along. Anyway it's not so simple to take off a curse.'

'But wouldn't you like to?' he urged her. 'Wouldn't you enjoy seeing the ballet? Doesn't it get a bit boring, sitting in this garden year after year, listening to all those jabbering nightingales?'

There was an indignant silence for a moment, then a chorus of loud, rude jug-jugs.

'Well –' she said at last, looking half convinced, 'I'll think about it. Won't promise anything. At least – I tell you what. I'll make a bargain. You fix about the church clock and the apology, I'll see what I can do about remitting the last bit of the curse.'

'Miss Collard,' said Rodney, 'you're a prime gun!' and he was so pleased that he gave her a hug. The wheel-chair shot backwards, Miss Collard looked very much surprised, and the nightingales all exclaimed,

'Phyooo – jug-jug-jug, tereu, tereu!'

Rodney climbed back over the wall with the aid of his rope. Mrs Sherborne had locked him out, so he spent the night more comfortably than he would have in her guest-room, curled up on a bed of hassocks in the church. The clock woke him by striking every quarter, so he rose at six forty-five and spent an hour and a half tinkering with the works, which hung down like a sporran inside the bell tower and could be reached by means of his rope.

'No breakfasts served after eight-fifteen!' snapped Mrs Sherborne, when Rodney appeared in her chilly parlour. Outside the windows mist lay thick as old-man's-beard.

'It's only quarter to,' he pointed out mildly. 'Hark!'

'That's funny,' she said, listening to the church clock chime. 'Has that thing gone bewitched, or have I?'

Rodney sat down quietly and ate his dollop of cold porridge, bantam's egg, shred of marmalade and thimble-ful of tea. Then he went off to the public call-box to telephone his fiancée Miss Tessa Prout (Porutska for pro-fessional purposes) who was staying at the White Lion Hotel in Bridport along with some other dancers and a camera team.

'Things aren't going too badly, love,' he told her. 'I think it might be worth your while to come over to Puddle. Tell the others.'

So presently in the Puddle High Street, where the natives were all scratching their heads and wondering what ailed their church clock, two large trucks pulled up and let loose a company of cameramen, prop hands, ballet chorus, and four dancers who were respectively to take the parts of the Student, the Girl, the Nightingale, and the Rose. Miss Tessa Porutska (née Prout) who was dancing the Nightingale, left her friends doing battements against the church wall and strolled along to Mrs Sher-borne's, where she found Rodney having a conversation with Fred.

'But Fred,' he was typing, 'I have passed on to you every fact in my possession. Surely from what you have had you ought to be able to locate this banana-peel dropper?'

'Very sorry,' creaked Fred, 'the programming is inadequate,' and he retired into an affronted silence.

'What's all this about banana-peel?' asked Tess, who was a very pretty girl, thin as a ribbon, with her brown hair tied in a knot.

Rodney explained that they needed to find a stage-hand who had dropped a banana-peel on the stage at Covent Garden thirty years before.

'We'll have to advertise,' he said gloomily, 'and it may take months. It's not going to be as simple as I'd hoped.'

'Simple as pie,' corrected Tess. 'That'll be my Great-Uncle Toby. It was on account of him going on all the time about ballet when I was little that I took to a dancer's career.'

'Where does your Uncle Toby live?'

'Just up the street.'

Grabbing Rodney's hand she whisked him along the street to the forge where the surly Mr Prout, ignoring the ballet chorus who were rehearsing a Dorset schottische in the road just outside his forge and holding up the traffic to an uncommon degree, was fettling a set of shoes the size of barrel-hoops for a great grey brewer's drayhorse.

'Uncle Toby!' she said, and planted a kiss among his white whiskers.

'Well, Tess? What brings you back to Puddle, so grand and upstage as you are these days?'

'Uncle Toby, weren't you sorry about the banana-peel you dropped that was the cause of poor Rose Collard breaking her leg?'

'Sorry?' he growled. 'Sorry? Dang it, o' *course* I was sorry. Sorrier about that than anything else I did in my whole life! Followed her up to London parts, I did, seeing she was sot to be a dancer; got a job shifting scenery so's to be near her; ate nowt but a banana for me dinner every day, so's not to miss watching her rehearse; and then the drabbited peel had to goo and fall out through a strent in me britches pocket when we was unloading all they unket rose-leaves on the stage, and the poor mawther had to goo and tread on it and bust her leg. Worst day's job I ever did, that were. Never had the heart to get wed, on account o' that gal, I didn't.'

'Well, but, Uncle Toby, did you ever *tell* her how sorry you were?'

'How could I, when she shut herself up a-grieving and a-laying curses right, left, and rat's ramble?'

'You could have written her a note?'

'Can't write. Never got no schooling,' said Mr Prout, and slammed down with his hammer on the horseshoe, scattering sparks all over.

'Here, leave that shoe, Uncle Toby, do, for goodness' sake, and come next door.'

Very unwilling and suspicious, Mr Prout allowed himself to be dragged, hammer and all, to the back of Rose Collard's garden wall. Here he flatly refused to climb over on Rodney's rope.

'Dang me if I goo over that willocky way,' he objected. 'I'll goo through the door, fittingly, or not at all.'

'But the door's stuck fast; hasn't been opened for thirty years.'

'Hammer'll soon take care o' that,' said Uncle Toby, and burst it open with one powerful thump.

Inside the garden the nightingales were all asleep; seamist and silence lay among the thickets. But Uncle Toby soon broke the silence.

'Rose!' he bawled. 'Rosie! I be come to say I'm sorry.'

No answer.

'Rose! Are you in here, gal?'

Rodney and Tess looked at one another doubtfully. She held up a hand. Not far off, among the thickets, they heard a faint sound; it could have been somebody crying.

'Rosie!' shouted Uncle Toby. 'Said I was sorry, didn't I? Can't do more'n that, can I?'

Silence.

'*Rosie*? Confound it gal, where are you?' And Uncle Toby stumped purposefully off among the thickets.

'Suppose we go and wait at the pub?' suggested Tess. 'Look, the sun's coming out.'

An hour later Mr Prout came pushing Miss Pollard's wheelchair along Puddle Fratrum's main street.

'We're a-going to get wed,' he told Rodney and Tess, who were drinking cider in the little front garden of the Haymakers' Arms. (It was not yet opening hours, but since the church clock now registered five a.m. and nobody could be sure of the correct time there had been a general agreement to waive all such fiddling rules for the moment.) 'A-going to get wed we are, Saturday's a fortnight. And now we're a-going to celebrate in cowslip wine and huckle-my-buff, and then my intended would like to watch a rehearsal.'

'What's huckle-my-buff?'

Huckle-my-buff, it seemed, was beer, eggs, and brandy, all beaten together; Tess helped Mr Donn (who was another uncle) to prepare it.

The rehearsal was not so easily managed. When the chorus of village maidens and haymakers were halfway through their schottische, a runaway hay-truck, suffering from brake-fade, came careering down the steep hill from Puddle Porcorum and ran slap against the post office, spilling its load all the way up the village street. The dancers only escaped being buried in hay because of their uncommon agility, leaping out of the way in a variety of jetés, caprioles, and pas de chamois, and it was plain that no filming was going to be possible until the hay had somehow been swept, dusted, or vacuumed away from the cobbles, front gardens, door-steps, and window-sills.

'Perhaps we could do a bit of filming in your garden, Miss Collard?' Rodney suggested hopefully. 'That would make a wonderful setting for the scene where the Nightingale sings all night with the thorn against her heart, while the Rose slowly becomes crimson.'

'I don't wish to seem disobliging,' said Miss Collard (who had watched the episode of the hay-truck with considerable interest and not a little pride; '*Well,*' she had murmured to her fiancé, 'just fancy my curse working as well as that, after all this time!') 'but I should be really upset if anything – well, troublesome, was to happen in my garden.'

'But surely in that case – couldn't you just be so kind as to remove the curse?'

'Oh,' said Rose Collard, 'I'm afraid there's a bit of a difficulty there.'

'What's that, Auntie Rose?' said Tess.

'As soon as you get engaged to be married you stop being a witch. Soon as you stop being a witch you lose the power to lift the curse.'

They gawped at her.

'That's awkward,' said Rodney at length. He turned to Tess. 'I don't suppose you have any talents in the witch-craft line, have you lovey, by any chance?'

'Well, I did just have the rudiments,' she said sadly, 'but of course I lost them the minute I got engaged to you. How about Mrs Sherborne?'

'The curse has to be taken off by the one who put it on,' said Rose.

'Oh.' There was another long silence. 'Well,' said Rodney at length, 'maybe Fred will have some suggestion as to what's the best way to put on a ballet with a company of one-legged dancers.'

They drank down the last of their huckle-my-buff and went along to Mrs Sherborne's.

'Hullo, Fred? Are you paying attention? We have a little problem for you.'

*

And that is why, when *The Nightingale and the Rose* was revived last year, it ran for a very successful season at Covent Garden danced by a company of one-legged computers, with Fred taking the part of the Nightingale.

A Jar of Cobblestones

SOME of you may know a town called Rye. In that town is a narrow, cobbled street, slicing up at an angle of thirty degrees from the dockside to the church. Mermaid Street, it's called, with the Mermaid Inn on the left near the top. And on the right, a little farther down, is this old haunted Jeake's House, built more than two hundred years ago by an astrologer. Well, one summer, exactly when I can't say, but not long ago, a young playwright called Julius Lapwing, who had been working in a sugar-beet factory all winter, found that he had earned enough money to rent a room in Jeake's House through the summer and write a play. So that is what he did.

The room he had was on the ground floor, looking out on to a little paved court with an old wooden swing in it. Ivy and jasmine swarmed over the windows, making the place rather dark. So the first thing Julius did was to paint the walls of his room white. No, first he had to scrub them with Swoosh; and in doing *that* he accidentally poked his scrubbing brush through a rotten board and found a little stone niche, like a fireplace without a chimney. And in the niche a big old green glass jar containing – would you believe it – six round flint cobblestones, each one the size of your fist. Rather nice and shiny they were, when Julius had washed the dust from them and put them, in their jar, on the window-sill, but he did wonder why somebody had taken the trouble to board them up in such a queer hideaway, what must have been many long years ago.

Well: at the end of a day's work the walls were white,

and so was the high ceiling, and Julius was tired out. But when he went to bed he found that his hands were sore and stinging, from the Swoosh detergent he had used to clean off the old paint. He tossed and fidgeted, he rubbed his hands with butter and then with calamine borrowed from his landlady. Still they burned and smarted. Then as he lay fretting his eye lit on the jar of big, smooth, cool cobblestones on the window-sill. Half asleep he staggered across the room, picked out a nice round stone, and tumbled himself back into bed, where he lay holding the beautiful heavy cold thing in both hands. And before he could count more than a sheep and a half, he had dropped asleep, straight into the middle of a dream.

It seemed to him that he was sitting out in the little paved court, with its smell of jasmine and ivy and snails. The moon was shining down, very bright. On the swing, basking in the moon's rays, idling herself to and fro by the tip of her tail, sat a mermaid. Julius was rather surprised to see her there, five miles and more from the sea, but being a polite young fellow he said Good evening and asked if she would fancy a cup of tea or a glass of cider. No thanks to that, Julius, she said, but I wouldn't refuse that cobblestone you're holding, it has old associations for me.

So Julius tossed her the stone, which she caught as if she had been wicket-keeping all her days, and, being a civil young chap, he asked her what the old associations were.

Two hundred years ago, said the mermaid, twiddling the swing back and forth with the tip of her tail, meanwhile tossing up the stone and catching it, very expert, two hundred years ago I had the misfortune to be netted by a family of mackerel fishers off Dungeness Point. And although I sobbed and pleaded, they wouldn't let me go, but fetched me into Rye on their donkey-cart and sold me

to the inn across the street from this house, and the inn-keeper hung me up for show, in a rope cradle that a sailor made for him.

That must have been uncomfortable, said Julius.

Painful, said the mermaid. Undignified too. And that wasn't the worst –

Julius was craning forward to hear what the worst was, but at that moment the church clock, a particularly loud one, struck seven and woke him; he was much surprised to find he had slept the whole night through. Even more surprised, hunting high and low among the blankets and bedding, to find never a trace of the sixth cobblestone!

Next night his hands were still giving trouble. And again, to cool them, he went to sleep clasping a round, cool cobble. And again he dreamed that he was out in his little court, chatting to the mermaid as she swung to and fro, playing toss-and-catch with the second stone.

The worst thing (she went on, as if there had been no interruption) was that just around that time there was an epidemic of pink-eye in the town. Somebody suggested it must be my fault. And in no time a mob was rushing up Mermaid Street shouting 'Get rid of the sea-witch! Take down the nasty magic thing and burn her!' Well! Just put yourself in my position. It had been vexatious enough to be strung up like a haddock in a rope cage, but the prospect of burning was a thousand times more disagreeable. And then they began pulling cobbles up out of the street and hurling them at me in a very rude way, bruising me all over my scales. However, just at that moment –

Just at that moment she broke off. The church clock was striking seven, and Julius woke up. Not a trace, any-where, of the second cobble.

What happened just at that moment? Julius asked next night when, in his dream, he had tossed the third cobble to the mermaid and she had caught it.

– Just at that moment the astrologer who lived in this house then – Samuel Jeake, his name was and he looked rather like you – he came out into the street, very cross. 'What's the meaning of all this row?' he asked. '*Must* you make such a noise just when I'm trying to calculate the influence of Pluto in Libra?' Then he caught sight of me and said, 'What are you doing to that unfortunate young person?'

'We're going to burn her,' one of the men said. 'She's a witch, and in her wicked malice she's given pink-eye to half the people in the town. Lower away, boys!'

'Rubbish! Superstitious nonsense!' said the astrologer. 'The pink-eye, as any person of education could tell you, was caused by a conjunction of Saturn in Libra sextile. And furthermore I can tell you, without even consulting my astrolabe, that if you burn this young marine female it will lead to disastrous consequences for the town – I can't specify exactly what without going into the matter more carefully, but it will be something in the nature of a flood, or maybe an earthquake.'

Well, that made them stop and think, and while they were thinking –

While she was speaking the church clock struck seven and Julius woke up.

What happened while they were thinking? he asked, tossing the fourth cobble to the mermaid on the fourth night.

Why, she said, catching it deftly with her left hand and giving the swing a shove off with her tail, while they were thinking, Samuel Jeake put half a dozen cobbles in his pockets and picked me up under one arm. 'She ought to be put back in the sea,' he said, and he took me into his house, slamming the front door. Very decent treatment he gave me then – set me out here to soak in a tub of water, for besides being bruised I was dangerously dry. Furthermore he sent his housekeeper out for a gallon of oysters for my supper, and had her rub me with mint from his garden; most refreshing.

'I must just do a bit of calculation, my child,' says he, 'it should be reckoned out tonight while the moon's in the house of Aries – then tomorrow I'll hire a donkey-cart and return you to your native element.' A very pleasant-spoken gentleman he was, uncommonly like you now I come to look at you.

Splashing in my tub out here I was quite contented, but in the middle of the night –

In the middle of her sentence the church clock struck seven and Julius woke up.

So what happened in the middle of the night? he asked next evening when he had thrown her the fifth cobble.

In the middle of the night, the mermaid said, some men from the town who weren't at all satisfied that I should be put back in the sea, for they wanted a witch-burning, these men came sneaking up the hill to Samuel Jeake's house. He was working away at his astrological calculations in the front room, and he heard them muttering and whispering. One of them softly tried the door.

'It's locked, boys – we'll have to go round the back. Climb over the garden fence,' a voice said.

When they had gone the astrologer came out to me. 'Now this is a nuisance,' he said. 'I fear these rough fellows are not to be influenced by zodiacal arguments. I think I shall be obliged to take you to the sea tonight – though I would have preferred to finish my calculations first.'

Lifting me out of my tub, he carried me into the house, up two flights of stairs and a ladder, out through an attic window, and on to part of the roof that was like a narrow gully between two sand dunes on Camber Strand. Here there stood a strange looking thing made from wood, and rope, and feathers, and metal that shone in the moonlight, and goodness knows what else.

'That's my flying machine,' said Samuel Jeake. 'I was going to try it out tomorrow, when I had made certain the stars were favourable, but as your affairs are somewhat pressing, my dear young sea-child, I shall have the trial flight tonight instead; it was built to carry a passenger and I do not suppose you weigh a great deal.'

He put me into a basket underneath one wing, and then glanced over the edge of the roof. Down below I could hear noises and crashes in the garden.

'I hope they do not trample on my mint bed,' said Samuel Jeake. 'Well, well, here we go,' and he climbed into the basket under the other wing, tossing out some of the cobblestones he had been using as ballast, and winding very hard on a wooden windlass.

Up went the machine, over the peak of the roof, over the garden, over the town wall. The wall, as you know, runs down steep as a cliff, to the River Rother, which circles the town. Tide was high, and I could see the water shining bright as my scales.

'This is capital!' says Samuel Jeake, winding away at his handle. 'In fifteen minutes we shall be at Rye harbour.'

But at that moment his machine began to tilt sideways. 'Humph,' said he, scratching his head. 'I really ought to have finished those calculations, I fear.' In spite of all his winding, we lost way altogether; the machine fell down, down, and crashed on the river bank. Luckily I was thrown into the water –

At that moment the church clock struck seven and Julius woke up.

He felt quite put out. He was impatient to hear the end of the story. It was plain that the mermaid must have escaped – presumably she had swum down the river to the sea. But what of the flying machine? And the astrologer? His speculations were interrupted by the arrival of a telegram. It said YOUR PLAY ACCEPTED COME TO MERMAID THEATRE THIS MORNING TO DISCUSS PRODUCTION.

Well! Julius was wild with excitement. He packed his toothbrush, his other pair of trousers, and the play he was working on, paid a month's rent to the landlady in lieu of notice, and rushed from the house. But he took the sixth cobblestone with him in his duffel-coat pocket. Some day, he thought, I'll come back and get her to tell me the end of that story. And he went running off to catch the London train, happy as a dog with a platinum tail.

It's not a common thing, after all, to hear that your play is being put on, *and* look forward to sharing a dream with a mermaid.

P.S. Samuel Jeake was a real astrologer, and he really did invent a flying machine and take off in it from the walls of Rye. The machine crashed but he escaped. Whether there was a mermaid on board I can't say, but he did live in the house halfway down Mermaid Street. I know because I was born in it.

A Long Day Without Water

THIS story is all about tears – tears locked inside a heart, heart lost in a river, river shut inside a house, house in a village that didn't want it. Better get out your handkerchiefs, then, for it sounds like a whole sky full of cloud coming along, doesn't it? And yet the ending, when we get there, isn't solid sad.

So listen.

Our village is called Appleby under Scar, and there's a river, the Skirwith Beck, that runs through the middle of it. Or did. Ran down the middle of the village green, chuckling and muttering among its rocks; clean-washed gravel-beds in summer on either side; in winter, of course, it was up to chest high, brown and foamy like the best oatmeal stout. In summer, days together, the children would be playing there, with dams, and stepping-stones, making castles on the sandbanks, picking up quartz stones, white, purple, and pink, all sparkling. A beautiful stream, the Skirwith Beck, the best kind. You can keep your willowy, muddy, winding rivers.

And the village green, on either side, was common land, villagers used to pasture their geese and donkeys there; lots of people used to have an old moke for when they wanted to go up on the fell and bring down a load of peat.

Summer evenings, half the village would be out on the green, enjoying the sunshine. There was a young fellow, Johnny Rigby, who had a little farm; hardly more than a smallholding, but he worked it hard and made a living from it; he was one of three brothers. Anyway this

Johnny Rigby was a rare lad for playing the fiddle and composing songs; he used to play his fiddle on the green, and the girls used to dance. Or everybody would gather round to listen if he'd made up a new song.

I can remember one of his to this day; kind of a catch, or round, it was:

> Standing corn, running river
> Singing wind, laughing plover
> Running fox, standing grain
> Leaping salmon, weeping rain
> Shining sun, singing lark
> Running roe, listening dark
> Laughing river, standing corn
> Happy village where I was born.

You see? It went round and round; pretty tune it had, still goes round and round in my head.

Johnny Rigby was friendly with a girl called Martha; nothing definite yet, but when he'd made up a new song, Martha would generally be the one that sat nearest to hear him sing it, and the first to get it by heart: Martha Dyson, pink cheeks and black hair, and bright dark eyes that saw further than most. Folks were pretty certain they'd get wed by and by.

Well, somewhere in among those long summer evenings of singing and chat on the Skirwith bank, some little chaps in glasses drove up to the village in a big Bentley car, and they were busy for days together, pottering about, taking samples of soil, poking instruments into the ground, weighing and measuring, peering about them through spyglasses, even getting down into the Skirwith Beck and taking samples of gravel from underneath *that*.

Nobody bothered about them. We're peaceable folk in these parts; if chaps don't worry us, we won't worry them. They used to eat their dinners in the Falcon pub, and we'd give them a civil good-day, but no more; we don't get thick with strangers all in a hurry round here; we give ourselves time to look them over first. And we had hardly given ourselves more than a couple of weeks to do that, when they were gone again, and then time went by and we forgot them.

But two or three months later – the hay was in and the harvest was half through – we heard what they'd been up to, and it was this.

It seems some big chemical firm – United Kingdom Alloys, the name was – had got wind there was a layer of mineral right under our village green, something quite uncommon and out of the way. Demetrium, it was called; a kind of nickel, Tom Thorpe told me it was, but that's as maybe. And the long and the short of it was, they wanted permission to dig up the green, or, in their language, opencast mine it, to a depth of fifteen feet.

Well! You can guess that stirred up a lot of talk in the village.

A few folk were dead against it, old Thunders Barstow for one. He was the sexton, and got his nickname from his habit of shouting 'The Lord shall send his thunders upon you,' when he didn't approve of something.

'What'll happen?' he said. 'They'll come here, wi' all their load of heavy digging equipment, they'll wreck the road from here to Paxton, carting yon stuff away, they'll make a right shambles o' the green; I shouldn't wonder if half the houses didn't tumble down because they'll undermine the foundations; they'll spoil the beck wi' their gravel and refuse, tha can say goodbye to t'trout and salmon, and then what? When they've got what they came for, they'll be off, leaving the place a fair wilderness.'

Of course United Kingdom Alloys promised and swore they would do no such thing. Every care would be taken of amenities, they said, in a letter on stiff crackly paper, the dug-out area would be filled in again and landscaped, all debris taken away, any damage made good, and so forth.

'Landscaped!' snorted old Thunders. 'What about our chestnuts? Tha cannot tweak up a two-hundred-year-old chestnut tree and set it back again as if it was a snowdrop bulb, sithee!'

Well, United Kingdom Alloys did admit they'd have to chop down the chestnuts – twenty of them, there were, all round the edge of the green – but they said they'd plant others, *mature trees*, they said, in another letter on even stiffer, cracklier paper, as soon as the work was completed.

'After all,' said Sam Oakroyd, 'there's no brass wi'out muck. And tha can see they mean to play fair by us.'

Brass, of course, was the nub of the business. U.K.A. were offering a right handsome sum for the use of our land – a figure that made most folk's eyes pop out on stalks when they heard it, though of course you had to remember it was going to be split up among the twenty people who owned the grazing rights on the green. And that was the hitch – everyone whose cottage faced on to the green had a say in the matter, and the firm couldn't so much as set a trowel into the ground till the whole twenty had agreed, as well as the Ministry of Town and Country Planning.

Well, the Ministry agreed – no argument there – and bit by bit everyone else did, as they realized what advantage it would bring them. Tom Thorpe could get a new farm truck, the Oakroyds would be able to send their daughter to music college, widow Kirby could get a modern stove put in her cottage, young Sally Gateshead could buy herself a hunter, the Bateses would be able to achieve their dearest wish, which was a colour telly, and the Sidebothams had set their heart on a holiday in

Madeira. One person who didn't agree was old Thunders Barstow, but his cottage didn't front on the green, so he had no say in the matter. And a lot of people thought old Thunders was a bit touched, anyway.

But just when everything seemed swimming along merrily and in a fair way to be fixed up, the whole scheme came to a stop because of one person.

That person was Johnny Rigby.

His two brothers had signed on the dotted line quick enough. Old man Rigby had died without making a will, and his farm had been split in three; there was just enough land for each brother, but you had to work hard to make it pay, and the two elder Rigbys, who shared the old man's house, though they weren't bone idle, weren't all that keen on work; they were fair tickled at the prospect of a nest egg from United Kingdom Alloys. Each brother owned grazing rights on the green, as Johnny had his own cottage, left him by his gran, and each had to agree before the company started work.

But Johnny wouldn't, and he was the last person in the village to make a stand.

He said it would spoil the place. He said no matter what was done afterwards, in the way of landscaping, Appleby would never be the same again. I think there was quite a few others agreed with him in their hearts, but they were overborne by their husbands – or wives – or children – who could see the benefits of hard cash, and were happy to let the future take care of itself.

Everybody argued with Johnny and tried to persuade him to change his mind. And as he wouldn't, the arguments grew more and more hot-tempered. People don't mince words in our parts.

'Tha stupid young milksop!' shouted old Sam Oakroyd. 'Tha'rt holding up progress and keeping good brass out o' folk's pockets, all for the sake of a moonshiny notion. A few trees and a bit o' rough pasture! Grass can be sown again, can't it?'

'And what about the river?' said Johnny. 'Can they put that back the way it was, after it's been taken out of its bed and run through a concrete pipeline?'

Johnny had fished and paddled and swum in the beck since he was out of his pram; he knew every rock and rowan tree along it, from Skipley to Paxton-le-Pool.

'Aye, they'll put it back – they said so, didn't they? Come on lad, don't be daft – just stop fussing and sign.' Old Oakroyd had the letter of acceptance, with everybody's names on it.

But Johnny wouldn't.

So there was a lot of ill-feeling against him. The Sidebothams said flat out that he must be mental, to refuse good cash, and ought to be committed to Skipley Home for Defectives. Tom Thorpe threatened to punch his head, several times his front windows were smashed, and I even heard someone let fly at him with a shotgun one night, as he came home on his motorbike from Paxton. There was no legal way he could be forced to change his mind, see; he had a right to his own point of view. The only person who stood by him was Martha Dyson.

'How are we going to get that thick-skulled brother of yours to change his mind?' Tom Thorpe said to Wilfred and Michael Rigby in the pub one night.

'I daresay he'll come round in time,' Wilfred said.

'Time! The firm won't keep their offer open for ever. There's big deposits of demetrium in Brazil, I read in the paper.'

'Then why the devil can't they *go* to Brazil for the stuff, 'stead o' scraping up our green to get tuppence-haporth out of it?' grumbled old Thunders.

'This is cheaper and handier for them, you silly old man.'

'Cheaper! Cheaper! The Lord shall call his thunders down on this pennypinching generation – aye, he shall give their flocks to hot thunderbolts,' declared the old man, who loved every stone of Appleby, and hated the thought of change.

Taking no notice of old Thunders, Wilfred Rigby said, 'The only way to get John to change his mind is by public boycott. He's always been a kind of a friendly, popular chap, with his fiddling and his songs; he'd feel it hard if nobody spoke to him, if nobody listened to his songs any more. That'd bring him round, I reckon.'

'Bring him round? It'd break his heart,' said old Thunders angrily. But no one took any notice of *him*.

So that was what they did. Nobody in the village would speak to Johnny. If he went into the pub, or the post office, folk turned their backs; if he strolled up to a group on the green, they all walked away.

Well, it's bitter hard for anybody in the world to have a thing like that happen to them – to be thrust out and given the cut by your own kin and neighbours – but for a song-writer it's worst of all. See, if you think about it, a song-writer needs folk to sing his songs *to*, he doesn't just make them up to sing into the empty air. It's like electricity: no connection, no current. Without friends to listen to his songs, and dance to his tunes, Johnny was like a fish without water to swim in, a bird without air to fly in; there just wasn't any point to him.

When it got too cold, in autumn-time, for musical evenings on the village green, Johnny'd been in the habit of holding a kind of open-house every Thursday evening. He hadn't much furniture in his cottage, for all the spare cash he had went on fertilizer and stuff for his land, but that made all the more room for friends. He had an old piano that had been his gran's, and anyone who liked could drop in for a bit of singing. If they brought a bottle of beer with them, all the better. Past winters, the house used to be chock full every Thursday, and people dancing in his patch of front garden too. He'd leave the door open, so the light would shine across the green, and you could hear the sound of fiddle and singing clear over the chuckle of the Skirwith Beck.

But not this autumn.

The first Thursday when it was too rainy and dark to linger outside, Johnny left his door open. It was pouring wet, and the sound of the beck was like a train running over points in the distance. The light from the door shone out, yellow on the rain. Martha was away, staying with her auntie in London, expected back next day. So Johnny was alone. He'd written a new song, and he played the tune softly on the piano, and louder on the fiddle; but nobody came. An hour went by, still nobody came. Johnny went outside in the wet and looked this way and that; no sign of anybody coming. But there was a light, and noise, from the Falcon pub, across the green, so he walked over. As he got closer he could hear voices singing and someone bashing the old pub piano; Mrs Ellie Sidebotham, it was, he saw when he got outside the window; her playing was enough to give you sinus trouble. But all the village seemed to be in there, singing and enjoying themselves.

Johnny pushed open the door and went in.

A dead silence fell.

Johnny nodded to Mr Baker, who kept the pub, and said he'd have a pint of bitter. Mr Baker couldn't refuse to serve him, so he did, but he didn't speak. Then Johnny took his drink and went over to the piano and pulled a bit of sheet music out of his pocket.

'I've written a new song, Mrs Sidebotham,' he said. 'Like to play it for me?'

Ellie Sidebotham was a silly, flustered kind of woman;

put you in mind of a moulting pullet. She didn't know how to refuse, so she started to play the tune, making a right botch of it.

And Johnny turned and faced the room, and began to sing.

> It's a long walk in the dark
> On the blind side of the moon
> And it's a long day without water
> When the river's gone –

But before he had sung any more than that, the bar had emptied. Folk just put down their drinks and left.

Ellie Sidebotham shuffled her way off the piano stool. 'I – I must be going too,' she said, and scuttled off.

Johnny looked round at the emptiness. He said, 'It seems I'm not welcome here,' and he walked out.

Wherever he went from the pub, he didn't go home till daylight; some folk said he just walked up and down the village green all night, thinking. In the morning he did go home, but that night's tramping up and down in the wet had done for him; big, strong chap as he was, he came down with a raging pneumonia, and when Martha got back from her auntie's in London and went along to see how he was, she found him tossing and turning on his bed with a temperature of a hundred and six. She ran to the pub and phoned for an ambulance to take him to hospital, but the Skirwith Beck was flooded and they had to take the long way round, and by the time they got there, Johnny was in a coma from which he didn't recover.

Folk felt pretty bad after his death, as you can guess.

There was a big turn-out for the funeral; the whole village came along, done up in black, looking respectful.

Appleby church stands on a kind of knoll above the village, opposite Martha's cottage. The knoll is an island when the beck's in spate, and it was in spate that day; it had rained solid ever since Johnny died. The footbridge was under water, so the only way to get to the graveyard was to row across. The vicar, Mr Haxley, was waiting on the other side. When all the mourners got to the river-bank, Martha Dyson came out from her cottage and faced them.

'You lot can just go home again,' she said. 'You didn't want my Johnny, and *you're* not wanted here. And if you want my opinion of you, you can have it – you're a lot of cowardly murderers, and you broke Johnny's heart among you, and I hope you're proud of yourselves.'

Not a soul had owt to say. They turned round, looking as shamed as dogs that have been caught sheep-worrying, and walked away through the rain. Martha Dyson and old Thunders began rowing the coffin across to the church. But the current was fierce, he was an old man and she only a bit of a lass; a huge eddy of flood water and branches came down on them and capsized the boat. Martha was a good swimmer, but she had her hands full with getting the old man to the bank; the vicar helped pull him out and the first thing was to get the pair of them dry and tended. By the time folk came to look for the boat and the coffin, neither could be found. The boat finally turned up, stove-in, down at Paxton-le-Pool. But the coffin with Johnny's body in it they never found, though the police dragged the Skirwith Beck clear down to where it joins the Ouse.

Well, you know how tales start up; it wasn't long before folk were saying the heart in Johnny's body had been so heavy with grief that it sank the boat.

But that wasn't the end of the matter, as you shall hear.

Of course, even if they pulled long faces, there were plenty of folk in the village who were relieved at Johnny's death, because now there was nothing to stand in the way of the United Kingdom Alloy scheme. His land went to his two brothers, and they had already signed the form.

So within two weeks the green was covered with bulldozers and those big grabbing machines that look like
nought in the world but prehistoric monsters, and they'd
cut down the chestnuts, and the grass on Appleby green
was a thing of the past.

Some folk were even mean enough to say, Wasn't it a
good thing that Johnny and Martha hadn't got wed yet –
they'd fixed to get married at Christmas, it came out –
because if she'd been his widow, instead of only his
intended, she'd have owned the grazing rights and been
able to withhold her permission. And there's no doubt
she would have. She was very bitter against the village.
Very bitter indeed, she was.

Those Rigby brothers must have felt guilty right down
to their socks for, believe it or not, when the U.K.A. paid
over the fee for use of land – which, fair play, they did
pretty promptly, though it turned out to be only half
what they'd said; the other half, they explained, would be
paid on completion of the operation – Wilfred Rigby went
along to see Martha Dyson. They hadn't spoken since the
funeral.

Martha's cottage, up the dale, opposite the church, had
been her family home from way back. Martha's grandmother had been a celebrated witch, or wise woman,
in her day, could charm warts and lay curses and make
prophecies; some folk said that Martha could too. Her
mother and father had died in the bad flood of '68, and
she lived on her own, kept bees, and sold the honey in
Paxton; did quite well out of it. She was feeding her bees
with sugar syrup when Wilfred came along. The beck
ran right past her gate, and there were two queer old
carved swans on the gateposts, asleep with their heads
under their wings – at least they were said to be swans, but
you could make them into pretty well anything you chose.

Wilfred had to clear his throat several times and finally

shout quite loud to attract Martha's attention; the beck was brawling away, still extra-high, and from the village there was a continuous grinding and roaring from the earth-moving machinery, and every now and then the ground would tremble as they dumped a big load of top-soil, or split a rock. By now, naturally, the whole village was a sea of slurry, and the road down to Paxton just a rutted, muddy watercourse.

'Well,' said Martha, hearing at last and turning round, 'what do *you* want?'

Wilfred – awkward and fumbling enough – went into an explanation of how – if by this time Martha had been married to Johnny – and if Johnny hadn't died – and if he'd agreed to the U.K.A. scheme – Martha would have come in for a bit of the brass. At last she understood him.

'You're offering me money?'

Wilfred shuffled his feet and brought out that, yes, he was.

'Why?'

He looked more uncomfortable still. He didn't like to admit that he was scared stiff of Martha's anger and wanted to soothe her down. He shuffled his feet again in the wet grass and said,

'We thought – Mike and I – that you might like to go on a bit of a holiday. Or – or the vicar was suggesting that as poor Johnny hasn't got a grave, we might wish to put up a memorial tablet to him. Maybe you'd like to use some of the money for that?'

Martha's eyes fairly blazed at him.

'You can just take your dirty money away from here, Wilfred Rigby, back to the mucky hole you've made of Appleby,' she said. 'I've got some brass of my own, that my gran left me, and I intend to put up my own memorial to Johnny. And I'd advise you not to try – there's some hypocrisy that even the wind and weather can't abide.

Any tablet *you* put up would crack in the first frost, it would get struck by lightning or washed away by a flood.'

'You're a hard, unforgiving woman, Martha Dyson,' said Wilfred.

'I've cause,' she snapped.

At that moment there was an extra loud crashing rumble from the village. And then Wilfred and Martha saw a queer and frightening thing. The Skirwith Beck, rushing down its rocky way, did a kind of sudden lurch sideways in its bed – just as a startled horse will shy at something ahead of it – the water lurched and rocked, and then, quick as I'm speaking, sank away out of sight, down into the ground.

'My lord! The beck! What's come to it?' Wilfred gasped.

'It's gone,' Martha said sombrely. 'Due to you and your money-grabbing mates it's gone. And I can tell you this, Wilfred Rigby – I shan't forgive you or anybody else in Appleby till it comes back again.'

And with that she turned her back on him and wouldn't speak any more and he was glad enough to hurry away.

Well, you can guess there was plenty more talk in the village about the lost beck. Some said it was due to natural causes – the vibrations from the heavy digging had likely cracked open an underground cavern, and the water had sunk through into it. But there were plenty believed it was the weight of Johnny Rigby's heavy heart that had sunk the river, as it had sunk the rowboat. And there were a few that thought Martha Dyson had done it, out of revenge against the village that had killed her Johnny. Martha never spoke to a soul in Appleby these days – except old Thunders – she bought her groceries in Paxton when she went with the honey.

Meanwhile the digging went on. Appleby looked like

some place in a war-zone that's had half a dozen battles fought in it, back and forth. And the beck never came back. Trees in gardens began to die, because their roots weren't getting enough water.

And Martha built her memorial to Johnny Rigby. She had a grand architect from London come down for the job, and a builder from York. It was a queer-looking thing enough when it was done – a little house in the churchyard, made of stone, with carvings on the outside all over – ears of wheat, birds, foxes, deer, fish, leaves, and what looked like ripples of water twining in and among and through all these things. It had a right unchancy feel about it – when you looked at it close enough you could swear the stone was moving, like grass waving or water running. There was a door at one end, and over the lintel Martha got the architect to put the two swans from her gateposts, with their heads under their wings.

On the side was carved the name John Rigby, and underneath some words:

... thou art cast out of thy grave like an abominable branch ...

For the waters of Nimrim shall be desolate: for the hay is withered away, the grass faileth, there is no green thing ...

Woe to the multitude of many people, which make a noise like the noise of the seas ...

And behold at eveningtide trouble; and before the morning he is not. This is the portion of them that spoil us, and the lot of them that rob us. (Isaiah XIV, XV, XVII.)

The vicar wasn't best pleased when he saw the words that had been carved, but Martha said they were Bible words, and by that time the architect and the builders had left, so in the end they were allowed to stay. There were a lot of complaints in the village about the tomb itself – folk said it was an outrage, and should be taken away. But the vicar put a stop to that.

Pretty soon there was a new tale in the village about this tomb.

The Bates family had a boy who wasn't quite right in the head. Simple Steve, or Silly Steve, he was called; the other children wouldn't play with him because he hardly ever spoke, but only made patterns on the ground with leaves and twigs and stones. It was a queer tale enough about him, and a sad one. Mrs Bates had had two boys, and was set on a girl for her next; when Steve was born, another boy, she wouldn't speak to him, kept him shut away in a back bedroom, and fed him only slops till he was six or seven. Lots of folk didn't even know he existed till the school attendance officer, doing a check, discovered that Steve ought to have been going to school for a couple of years and couldn't even speak. There was a fuss, threats of prosecution, but in the end it died down. Steve was sent to school, but he didn't learn much. The teacher was very angry about it all, and said he wasn't really simple; if he'd been cared for and spoken to properly from the start it would have been all right; but it was too late now. Well, there you are; that's the kind of thing you find even in families that seem quite normal and above-board.

Simple Steve used to spend quite a lot of time in the graveyard, playing his pattern-games on the flat tomb-stones. Old Thunders didn't mind him; in fact the two got on quite well; they could make themselves understood to each other in a kind of sign language. Steve used to help cut the grass and clip the hedges. The old man would whistle as he worked and Steve, though he could hardly talk, could hum a tune; old Thunders taught him some of Johnny Rigby's tunes. But there was one corner of the graveyard Steve would never go near, and that was where Johnny Rigby's memorial stood; he explained to the old man that he was afraid of the tomb because the beck was all shut up inside that little house, and one day it was going to break out and flood all over the village. By and by somehow this tale got round, and although they knew it was nonsense, a lot of folk half believed it, specially the children.

Nobody could get inside; Martha kept the key of the locked door; she said, if ever Johnny's coffin was found, it should be put in. On a bright sunshiny afternoon it used to be a dare game for the braver kids to go and listen at the keyhole. They'd come away quaking and giggling, declaring they could hear the beck running inside – like when you put your ear to a shell. Not one of them would have had the nerve to go near the place at night.

By this time the winter was nearly over. Frost and snow hadn't stopped the U.K.A. – they'd been digging away like badgers all through. There had been one or two mishaps – a few people fell into the diggings at night and broke legs or arms; the works were taken a bit too near the Rigby brothers' house and it collapsed, but they weren't killed, and the U.K.A. swore they'd pay compensation. Also they cut through the village water-supply and sewage system, but the Public Health lot made them put the sewer right pretty quick, before they had a typhoid epidemic on their hands. The Rigbys weren't so lucky; they hadn't got their compensation by the time the U.K.A. people left, nor had Thorpe, for his collapsed barn, nor the Bateses for their garden which had sunk down ten feet, nor widow Kirby, who'd had twelve ton of subsoil accidentally dumped on hers. And there were various other troubles of the kind, but people reckoned the company would pay for these things at the same time as they paid the second half of the fee for use of land.

Well, the excavators left, and took their machinery with them, leaving the place like the crater of a volcano; and folk were beginning to wonder when the landscapers would be along with their turf, and mature trees, and whatnot, to make good the devastation, fill in the excavated area, and carry out all their promises.

It was at this point that we read in the papers about the United Kingdom Alloy Company going bankrupt.

Over-extended its resources, was the phrase used in court when the case was heard.

They'd had irons in too many fires, borrowed cash here to pay for operations there which turned out less successful than they'd hoped; and the outcome of the matter was they'd gone into liquidation, paid sixpence in the pound to their creditors, and the head of the firm had disappeared, thought to have absconded to Brazil to escape all the trouble he'd left behind him.

And as for our mature trees, topsoil, turf, compensation, and the Skirwith Beck, we could whistle for them.

You'd hardly believe what happened next.

Martha Dyson still wasn't speaking to anyone in the village. People said she was so bitter, even the birds and the wild animals kept away from her garden. But one day a deputation from the village went to call on her: Mrs Kirby, Mrs Bates, Tom Thorpe, and the Sidebothams. They stood inside Martha's gate looking nervous till she came out and asked them what they wanted. They all hummed and ha'd and looked at one another, until at last Ellie Sidebotham burst out with it.

'We've come to ask you to take the curse off!'

'Curse, what curse?' Martha says.

'The curse you put on the village! We've no water-supply, the trees and plants are all dying, the green's just a hole full of shingle – there's no end to the trouble. Oh, Miss Dyson, do please take it off. We're scared to think what might happen if it gets any worse!'

At that Martha laughed, a short, scornful laugh.

'You poor fools, *I* didn't put any curse on you,' she said. 'It was your own short-sighted greed put you in this mess, and you'll just have to get yourselves out of it as best you can.'

'But you said to Will Rigby that until the Skirwith Beck came back –'

'I said I shouldn't forgive you till then, and it's true, I shan't. Now go away and leave me in peace,' Martha said.

'Then you're a hard, heartless woman, Martha Dyson!' squeaked Ellie Sidebotham. 'And with all your memorials and show of mourning Johnny Rigby I don't believe you've ever shed a tear for him!'

White-faced and dry-eyed Martha glared at her. Then she said,

'Get out of my garden. And you can tell the rest of them, down in the village, that if anyone else comes here without being asked, I *shall* get out my grandmother's book of curses.'

They cleared out pretty quick at that, and went back to the village muttering. As for Martha, she sat down on her doorstep, sick with sadness, and shivering, shivering cold. For it was true, since Johnny's death, she hadn't been able to cry; not a tear.

Well, the people of Appleby saw they'd get no help from Martha, and they found they'd get none, either, from the Ministry of Town and Country Planning, which said it might be able to do something for them in a couple of years but not sooner. So they realized they'd have to help themselves, and they clubbed together and started a fund for Village Beautification. The Bateses reckoned they could do without their colour TV another year, Sally Gateshead sold the new hunter, the Sidebothams fixed to go to Blackpool instead of Madeira. And so on. Furthermore they arranged a rota of working parties to start getting the green back into shape. The trouble was fetching down enough topsoil from the fells to fill in the hole; that was going to take a lot of men a lot of time.

However they'd hardly got started when the cold came on, very severe.

Up to then it had been an unusually mild winter, for our parts. But in late March, after a specially warm spell, there was a sudden real blizzard. First it thundered, then it hailed, then the snow came down solid white, out of a black sky. And the snow went right on for twenty-four hours, till all you could see of Appleby were a few humps, the roofs of houses, and the church spire on its knoll. The shallow crater in the middle of the village was filled with snow, and looked decenter than it had for many a week. There were no trees above the snow; what hadn't been chopped had all fallen during the winter.

We're well used to snow, of course; so folk who hadn't beasts to tend stayed in and kept snug. At least there was plenty of firewood: chestnut wood. But in the middle of the night following the storm, all of a sudden there came the loudest noise you can imagine; some thought it was the H-bomb, others that the top of Skipley Fell had come loose and slid down in an avalanche.

Well, it was a kind of avalanche, they discovered in the morning. The bottom of the crater that had been Appleby Green had fallen in, due to the weight of snow piled in it, and the crater was now a whole lot deeper; but before they had time to discover how much deeper, it filled up with water. For the sudden cold had turned to a sudden thaw; the snow was melting as fast as it had come.

That morning Martha was looking over her bee-hives, to make sure they'd taken no hurt in the snow, when she saw a black procession of men going up to the church, carrying something shoulder-high.

Mr Haxley the vicar came over and tapped on Martha's gate. His face was solemn, and he looked as if he didn't know how to begin what he had to say. But she got there first.

'They've found him?'

'Yes, my dear. I've come to ask for the key.'

Seemingly all that rock and snow and rubble, crashing down through the bottom of the crater, must have filled up the underground chamber again, or blocked the entrance, and in doing so it had floated up Johnny Rigby's coffin, on the melted snow-water, from where it had been lodged underground. It was found beached on the edge of the pool that had been Appleby Green.

Martha gave the key to Mr Haxley. But the men found they didn't need it, for the end of the empty tomb, and the tree that stood nearest to it, had both been struck by lightning in the storm the night before. The end wall of the tomb had fallen away, and the door was all charred.

The men of the village, who had carried Johnny's coffin up, laid it inside the tomb while the vicar read the funeral service, and then they rebuilt the wall and set in a new door. But they couldn't find the two stone swans, which seemed to have been clean destroyed. All that time, Martha watched them from her garden gateway. When they were leaving she made them a kind of bow, to signify she was grateful for what they'd done. And when they'd gone, she sat down on her doorstep, threw her apron over her head, and cried as if a dam had burst inside her.

But that day wasn't over for Martha yet. After a while, as she sat there grieving, but more gently now, she heard a sound by her. She pulled the apron off her face, and found the little Bates lad, Simple Steve, sitting on the step next to her, quiet-like, making one of his patterns with sticks and leaves.

'Hallo!' she said, fair astonished, for no kid from the village ever set foot inside her garden.

He gave her a nod, and the kind of grunt that was all he'd do for hallo. And went on with his pattern. It was a peaceful kind of thing to watch, and presently she got to

helping him, handing him bits of stuff, and showing him
where he could make the pattern better.

Steve began humming to himself as he often did.

'Where did you learn that?' asked Martha, startled.
For the tune was one of Johnny's.

Steve nodded his head sideways, towards the churchyard over the way, meaning, probably, that old Thunders
had taught it him.

Martha took up the tune with him, singing the words.

> It's a long walk in the dark
> On the blind side of the moon
> And it's a long day without water
> When the river's gone
> And it's hard listening to no voice
> When you're all alone.

Steve learned the words from her, after his fashion, and
he began singing them too.

'You sing well, Steven,' she told him.

At that, Steve's face did a thing it had never done
before. It smiled. Then he pointed past Martha. She
turned, and saw that an old tail-less black cat, Mrs
Kirby's Tib, had come into the garden. And that wasn't
all. There were rabbits, and a stray ewe, a young fox, even
a roe-deer, had all pushed their way through the hedge.

'Mercy, what's come over the creatures?' said Martha,
more and more amazed.

'They know the beck's coming,' said Steve nodding. 'I
did, too.'

She understood what he meant, then. In the bad flood
of '68, only Martha's cottage and the church knoll stood
above water level.

'I'd best warn them,' she said. 'You stay here, Steve.'

And she walked quickly down to Appleby, where half
the village was out, gazing at the pool that had been

Appleby Green. They gawped when they saw Martha, as
you can guess.

'I've come to tell you the beck's coming down,' she
said. 'You'd best – you'd best come up to my place.'

They didn't hang about. In our parts we know how,
when the snow melts up on the high fells, a little trickle of
water can turn to a raging torrent in ten minutes. Tom
Thorpe went round, shouting them out of their houses,
and they were up at Martha's, carrying all they could,
almost as quick as I'm telling it. And only just in time, too,
for the Skirwith Beck came thundering down the dale only
a few minutes after, as if it were carrying the troubles and
quarrels of the whole village on its back.

They had to stay up at Martha's for three hours, while
the water raged through the village. She made them cups of
tea, and so forth, while the women helped, and they all
shared out what food they'd brought with them. Then
the water went down – it's fast come, fast go, up here –
and they went back to look at the damage.

Well, it wasn't too bad. The houses are solid-built, they
were all right; of course there was a lot of mud and wet
that would want cleaning out. Everybody set to, right
off, scrubbing and lighting fires and airing. But the
wonderful thing was that in its wild spate the beck had
fetched down enough peat and loam and topsoil from the
high fell to cover the ugly stony crater the United
Kingdom Alloy Company had left behind them. There
was still a small, deep round pool in the middle; the beck
had made a new course for itself, ran in one side and out
the other.

Two swans were swimming about on the pool. No one
knew where they had come from.

It was all hard work, after that, for months. Getting the
dirt evenly spread, making a new pathway round the
green, paving it with flat stones, and sowing grass. What-

ever was done, Martha Dyson was there, helping. With
the Beautification Fund they bought young chestnut trees
from a nursery and set them round the way the others
had been.

'Reckon they ought to see our grandchildren's grandchildren out,' Tom Thorpe said.

Young Steve Bates went to live with Martha. He just
wouldn't leave her house, when the others went back after
the flood. Mrs Bates raised no objections and Martha
said she'd like to adopt him. He did better with his book-
learning, after, though he'd never make Skipley Grammar.
But he started learning the fiddle, and he was handy at
that.

Well, Johnny Rigby was right in one thing he said.
He'd said that, no matter what happened afterwards,
Appleby would never be the same again. And it isn't. But
maybe in some ways it's better.

The Prince of Darkness

ONCE there was a clever lazy boy called George who worked in a lab. His job was to take all the odds and ends left lying around after the manufacture of books and bicycles and bread and buttons and bathroom fittings, and mix them together in the hope of making something useful from the leftovers.

Well, one day, shaking up this and that in a test-tube, George produced a quite unexpected result: after a brown seething, and a hissing, and a puff of black smoke inside the glass tube, he found that it contained a tiny person with a crown and sceptre and a forked tail: the Prince of Darkness, in fact.

'Fancy,' said George, but without too much surprise, for he had always expected to do something as clever as this one day. And he tipped the devil out on to the scrubbed wood of the laboratory bench.

'Thanks,' said Lucifer, shaking off the last drops of the brown fluid.

Next minute George had clapped a bell-jar over him.

The devil banged furiously on the side of the jar.

'Let me out!' he shouted.

'Only if you do something for me.'

'This is all the wrong way round,' said Lucifer. 'I ought to have your signature in blood first.'

'Well, you haven't got it,' said George, whistling, and he washed his hands, turned off all the lights, and began shutting up the lab for the night.

The devil finally gave in; he knew a really obstinate nature when he met it.

'All right,' he said, 'what do you want?'

'I want you to make my fortune.'

'That's easy,' said Lucifer. 'I'll arrange for someone to call on you tomorrow.'

George lifted the bell-jar and the devil fluttered out like a moth.

At ten o'clock next morning (it was a Saturday) George was frying herrings for his breakfast over the oil-stove in his cottage when a fox leapt through his kitchen window crying, 'Save me! Save me! The hounds are coming.'

'But you steal chickens,' said George.

'I've never stolen any of yours.'

'True,' said George, who had no chickens. 'But won't the hounds notice your scent?'

'The herrings will drown it.'

'All right,' said George, 'you can hide in the bathroom.' And he shut the door on the fox just as the South Surrey Hunt, in full cry, hounds, master, whippers-in, followers, and members of the Pony Club, came pelting into his garden.

'Hey, you,' said the Master, 'have you seen our fox in your garden?'

'No,' said George truthfully, 'and you're making the devil's own mess of it.'

Several of the hounds surged into the kitchen, but George fobbed them off with scraps of herring, and the hunt roared off into the woods behind the cottage.

'You can come out now,' George called, but the fox was having a bath and took his time about it.

'I never gave you permission to use my after-shave lotion,' George said, when he did come out.

'I thought it would disguise my scent,' the fox replied, lying down in front of the fire to dry. 'Now, give me a bit of breakfast, and then I'll help you make your fortune.'

So George fried a few more herrings (luckily he bought them by the half-cran).

'Right,' he said, when the fox had made a hearty meal. 'Now what?'

'Now you must paint a sign saying ANYTHING MENDED. While it dries you can write a letter of resignation to the lab. Then stick up the sign on your front gate.'

So George washed up and did these things while the fox rolled over luxuriously on to his back, so as to dry the other side.

The paint was hardly dry and the sign hardly in position before people began ringing George's doorbell.

You know how hard it is to get anything mended. Shoes, clocks, TV sets, Ming vases, Chippendale chairs, broken hearts – you'll be lucky if you can find a cobbler or a watchmender within twenty miles, a man who'll repair your Stradivarius violin within twenty months. And as for some broken hearts, they never get mended at all.

So within twenty-four hours George was doing a roaring trade, and had to turn away as many customers as he accepted. He worked like a beaver, without even a break for a cup of tea, mending one thing after another at top speed, while the fox reclined in front of the fire and gave him his instructions.

At the end of six months George was rich enough to buy up the whole of Alaska, or to travel round the world, if there had been time. But there wasn't.

'Look here!' he complained one day. 'I asked the devil to make my fortune. I didn't expect to be worked to death.'

'You should have worded your wish more carefully,' said the fox, shrugging, and tossing a couple of logs on to the fire. (George kept meaning to have central heating installed, but there wasn't time for that either.)

After another six months George took a day off and went back to the lab, where a friend of his let him borrow a test-tube and a retort and some crucibles and a private corner where he wouldn't be disturbed. For all this time he had carefully hung on to the formula which produced the brown fluid.

Well, it worked again. The liquid seethed and hissed, like tea gone wild, there was a black puff, a white vapour, and, all of a sudden inside the test-tube George saw the tiny Prince of Darkness, shaking his fist, looking very annoyed at being caught twice.

This time George didn't let him out of the tube, but clapped in a cork, stuck the tube in his jacket pocket, thanked his lab-friend, and started for home. He wanted to ask the advice of the fox, who was very clever, if lazy, before he made his next wish.

On the way home George stopped in at the village grocery store to buy tinned herrings (he and the fox had taken to eating these instead of the fresh kind because they were quicker to serve).

There was an old boy called Mr Mudgwick doddering about the crowded, inconvenient little shop, putting bread and beans and bacon and brown eggs and butter and biscuits and Brie and Bovril and bullybeef and Banbury cakes into a basket; he was the postman and lived at the end of the village and had a pretty niece called Ellie, and George knew him slightly.

'How do, Mr Samson,' said the postman, bumping George on the hip with his basket of groceries. 'I've an old radio set that do need fixing terrible bad. Can I bring her along to your place?'

'All right,' said George with a sigh. The sight of all the different and delicious foods in Mr Mudgwick's basket had reminded him what a boring and monotonous diet he and the fox were confined to. 'Tell you what,' he went on, brightening, 'why don't I come round and fetch your radio? Those old sets can be pretty heavy.'

For he hoped that he might be invited to supper.

Mr Mudgwick agreed to this, and went off with his basketful. He also, though George did not realize this at the time, went off with the test-tube. In his young days Mr Mudgwick had been a professional pickpocket, and though he no longer picked pockets for a living, he did like to do one from time to time 'just to keep me hand in,' as he pleaded to his niece, who was very cross about it. 'I knows it ain't that I needs to, now I've got me postman's screw coming in regular, but it's just the interest, Ellie; I does like to know what folk has in their pocketses.'

'It's downright disgraceful, Uncle Tom,' Ellie said indignantly. 'And look at all the trouble you give me, returning the things you've pinched from folk.'

Luckily all the people round about were very easy-going; they made allowances for Mr Mudgwick's little way, because Ellie was so obliging and pretty and always gave them a pot of her honey or home-made blackberry jelly when she returned the stolen articles. But sometimes it was difficult to know who the things belonged to, if Mr Mudgwick had taken several, and if the grocer's shop had been crowded so that he was not sure whose pocket they had come from.

In the present case Ellie recognized a silver cigarette lighter in the shape of a hunting-horn, which belonged to the Master of Foxhounds, and a bag of mothballs, which belonged to old Mrs Liddell, who was afraid of moths setting upon her and devouring her clothes in the village street, but the test-tube with the little furious royal character inside it had her stumped, when she did her usual sort-through of the contents of Uncle Tom's pockets after tea.

'Blest if I can remember, Ellie, me dear,' the old man confessed when she asked him. 'Me memory's getting desprit bad these days. It was some young feller as I ran into at the grocer's, that's all I know.'

There was nothing for it but to pull out the cork and ask the person inside the test-tube, so this Ellie did.

Lucifer was not at all pleased. He shot up to a hundred feet high, throwing off jet-black sparks and rays of night.

'I am the Prince of Darkness, and I belong to no one but myself,' he said angrily.

'I only asked,' said Ellie. 'I didn't mean to hurt your feelings. I wish you'd come down, it's rather difficult talking to you up there. Besides, you've made a hole in the roof.'

Lucifer had the grace to apologize. He came down to human height, mending the hole on the way, which was just as well, for the thatch was beginning to smoulder.

'Now, what can I do for you?' he asked. 'I owe you a good turn for getting me out of that test-tube.'

'That's kind of you,' Ellie said, 'but we're fairly comfortable, with Uncle's salary and my bees and jam; I don't reckon there's anything we need.'

'But I ought to grant you a wish,' said the devil, rather taken aback.

'Well, these things don't always turn out for the best, do they?' Ellie pointed out comfortably. 'I think we'll go on as we are.'

'I could change your uncle's nature so that he didn't pick pockets any more.'

'He might do something worse, then, mightn't he? Or go all bad-tempered and grumpy, which I couldn't abide. It's safer to leave him as he is. Now, if you wouldn't mind telling me whose pocket you came out of, just so's I can explain matters.'

Just then George arrived to collect the radio. He had

been very put out, on returning home, to find the test-tube gone from his pocket. Keeping so busy with his work, George had next to no chance to hear village gossip and was unaware of Mr Mudgwick's little failing, so he had no notion who could have taken the tube. He was therefore delighted to see Lucifer in Ellie's kitchen and made a grab for him, which the devil easily evaded, shooting up the chimney in a cloud of sparks.

'Oh dear,' said Ellie, 'did the tube belong to you, then? What a shame. I *am* sorry. Uncle is so thoughtless. Never mind, sit down, as you're here, and have a bit of supper. I've been making corned-beef hash.'

Ellie's hash was so delicious that George forgave her uncle.

'Anyway, I still have the formula,' he said. 'I'll mix it up again some time, when I've a slack day from the mending.'

Slack days were very few, though. People now sent George things to be mended from all over the world: electric kettles, magic carpets, racehorses with broken legs, nuclear-powered submarines, dishonoured treaties, computers with mental breakdowns. It was quite a while before he managed to get round to mending old Mr Mudgwick's radio; he didn't even have time to go back for another dish of Ellie's delicious hash, though she had invited him to drop in for supper whenever he liked.

Meanwhile Ellie and her uncle were in trouble. Not about the pocket-picking; much worse. A new bypass road was to be taken past the village, and the transport people planned to put a large roundabout right where Mr Mudgwick's cottage now stood; Ellie and her uncle were given a month's notice to quit.

Mr Mudgwick was thunderstruck. 'What, leave the house where I've always lived, and me granfer's grand-father afore me? No one's going to get me out.'

'You'll be paid compensation,' the official from the Ministry for the Environment told him.

'Compensation's not the same as me own fireplace where I've toasted cheese for seventy year,' said Mr Mudgwick. 'Besides, compensation ain't enough to buy a rat hole, let alone a dog kennel. They can send the minister himself, I ain't budging.'

They did send the minister himself, Lord Motorway. By that time, George had got round to repairing old Mr Mudgwick's radio and had brought it back. It was working as well as ever. But the programmes on it were the programmes of forty years ago.

When the minister, a distinguished-looking silver-haired man, came through the door of Mr Mudgwick's cottage and heard the songs of his childhood, great tears came into his eyes and rolled down his cheeks.

'Oh,' he sighed, 'that takes me back to when I was a young lad and lived at Walton-on-the-Naze. I'll pay you any sum you care to name for that radio.'

'Not likely,' declared old Mr Mudgwick. 'Part with me radio what I've been a-listening to since I was an Ovaltiney? Not likely!'

'But, Uncle Tom,' said Ellie, 'if Lord Motorway wants it as much as that, he might pay us enough to buy a nice cottage somewhere else.'

'A nice cottage somewhere else ain't the same as me own here,' said Mr Mudgwick.

The minister went back to London, declared that people ought to be left in their homes in peace and, as the Prime Minister did not agree with him, resigned from his post. Another minister was appointed who didn't care a snap of his fingers about the songs of forty years ago. He ordered the construction firm to start work on the road and the demolition firm to start work on Mr Mudgwick's cottage. A great ring of machines like dinosaurs came and stood in a cluster in the garden, while the bypass inched its way closer and closer. But, just the same, the work went badly. Great cracks kept appearing in the tarmac, the banks crumbled as soon as they were built, and the cats'-eyes sank down through the white line and disappeared for ever.

'You'd think there was a curse on this job,' grumbled the new minister.

'They say there's a young chap lives in the village as is wonderful clever at mending things,' said the foreman of the construction firm. 'Maybe he'd be able to put the road to rights.'

They asked George if he could mend the road.

'Not unless you bring it here,' he said. 'I only mend things in my workshop.'

So they had to prise up the new road, all twenty miles of it, roll it up, and cart it along to George's cottage on twenty trucks. He said he'd do it as soon as he could get round to it; he was very busy just then.

Ellie went for a walk in the woods, and her heart was full of trouble and worry, so that her eyes were blurred with tears and she could hardly see where she was going. Tripping over an oak-root she put out a hand to save herself and found that, instead of catching hold of a branch, she had grabbed on to the antler of a great black stag with fiery eyes. She recognized him directly and managed to give him a civil nod; her throat was too tight with tears for conversation.

'Well,' said the Prince of Darkness, 'do you want to tell me your trouble, Miss Ellie?'

'Oh,' she gulped out then, 'it's not so bad for me, I'm young, and I daresay I'd have left home and moved away one day anyway, but poor old Uncle Tom! Any minute now they're going to start knocking down our cottage, if they haven't begun already.'

'Eh, dear,' sighed Lucifer, 'I thought that George had a big-headed nature, but your Uncle Tom is even worse. Gracious knows I've done my best to help you. What an obstinate set of souls you are in these parts. Well, Miss Ellie, are you still too proud to accept that wish?'

Ellie thought it over and said she'd be pleased for him to help her. After all, he did owe her a kindness, and it was for the old man's sake.

So the black stag stamped with his foot on the mossy ground, the sky darkened, and there was a loud clap of thunder.

'Best go along to George's cottage now,' said Lucifer. 'There's one thing I *can't* do for you; you'll have to make your own arrangements about that; but tell George to get in touch with one of his nine uncles and he'll be able to do the job for you.'

Ellie couldn't think what in the world Lucifer meant, but she thanked him very politely and ran through the wood towards home.

When she reached the spot where Uncle Tom's cottage ought to have been, she stopped in astonishment, for it wasn't there.

Everybody else seemed quite surprised too. The ring of dinosaurs hung their heads and looked foolish, as if they were hungry and could find nothing to snap up in their great jaws. All the construction and demolition men stood scratching their heads and leaning on their pickaxes.

'Lawks, Miss Ellie,' one of them said, 'your cottage has just sailed off, dear knows where. A black whirlwind came roaring along and snatched it away.'

'I can guess where it's gone,' Ellie cried joyfully, and she ran to the other end of the village. Sure enough, not far from George's little house stood old Mr Mudgwick's thatched cottage, slightly skew to the road as if it had been dumped down rather carelessly; Uncle Tom was

just coming slowly out of the front door, staring about
him in a puzzled manner.

' 'Tis a pernicious long way from here to the pub,' he
grumbled. 'Whether I go to the Ring o' Roses or the
Black Swan, a tedious long way it be. Why the pize
couldn't they let us bide where we've allus resided?'

George left off repairing a picture by Velasquez, worth
gracious knows how many thousand pounds, to come out
of his cottage and bid them welcome.

'Now we're such close neighbours I hope you'll come
and have a taste of my hash a bit oftener,' Ellie said
happily. Then she remembered Lucifer's message about
George's nine uncles, and asked him what he thought it
meant.

'Ah,' George said, 'you'll be needing a well. Lucifer
may be able to pick up a cottage like a walnut and sail it
through the air, but even he can't transplant running
water. My nine uncles are all water-diviners; I'll send a
message for Uncle Matthias, he's the nearest.'

Uncle Matthias was pleased to come over next Sunday
in his rickety three-wheeled invalid car (as supplied by the
Ministry of Social Security, for he was lame and rheu-
maticky from hanging over springs all the year long)
bringing with him his forked hazel stick.

'It's a terrible hard-working life, being a water-
diviner,' said George. 'That's why I went into a lab.'

In spite of his rheumatism, Uncle Matt was a gay little
man, who dearly loved unearthing water; in his time he
had found springs all over the world, from Euston Station
to the Spanish Steps, and before they could check him
he had located half a dozen springs in the village, one in
the middle of the High Street, one in front of the post
office, one in Mr Mudgwick's new garden, and a spare
one where the road builders could happily have done
without it, in Mr Mudgwick's old garden, which was

now the circular centre of a traffic roundabout. Here a
mighty fountain suddenly burst through the ground,
soaked all the men and their machines, and continued
spouting like a geyser, no matter what efforts were made
to stop it.

The new Minister for the Environment was summoned,
to come and see for himself all the disasters that were
afflicting his road works.

'Where's the road?' was the first question he asked.

'It's away being mended, Sir Bruce. The repair tech-
nician has told us it won't be ready for six months.'

(The fox had told George to say this; in fact he could
have mended it faster if he had really applied himself to
it.)

The new minister, Sir Bruce Bypass, became very dis-
couraged. 'I can see old Motorway had a bit of sense in
his view that this wasn't the best spot for a new high-
way,' he said. 'Maybe we'd better give up this project and
take our plans elsewhere.'

So they packed up their picks and kerbstones and cats'-
eyes, trundled away their bulldozers and concrete mixers,
revved up their motors, and all departed, leaving a brand-
new roundabout with a fountain in the middle of it, and
twenty miles of rolled-up dual carriageway in George's
back garden.

Old Mr Mudgwick was annoyed about the whole
thing.

'Now I gotta walk the length of the village to get me
pint of old and mild,' he grumbled. 'Why the blazes
couldn't they leave us where we was?'

George was discontented too. Although he was delighted to have Ellie so near at hand, baking batches of
buns and frying her savoury hash, people still kept
bringing more and more things that needed mending, and
he wished he didn't have to work quite so hard.

So one day he left Ellie kindly mending a magic carpet for him and cycled along to the lab, with his precious formula on its grubby scrap of paper. His friend obliged him with a corner and a filter-paper and a test-tube, he shook up the brown mixture as before, and as before there was a puff and a cloud of smoke and a seething pop.

'Oh, no, my friend!' said Lucifer, bursting his way out of the glass tube. 'Nobody catches the Prince of Darkness three times. Not even such a clever boy as you.' One of his fingers flared up like a bunsen burner, and before George could save it, the precious formula had shrivelled to a sooty wisp. Lucifer turned into a black hook-eared owl and flew out through the window, upsetting two carboys full of acid and puncturing the tyres of George's bicycle, so George had to walk home, very disgruntled.

Meanwhile Ellie, having put a neat patch into the carpet, took it across to George's cottage and looked round to see if there was anything else she might be able to mend.

The first thing she saw was the fox, snoozing in front of the fire.

'Hullo!' she said, recognizing him at once.

'Hullo, Ellie,' said Lucifer. 'How are things going at home?'

'Uncle Tom doesn't like being so far from the pub.'

'One could work to the end of one's life and still not satisfy you people,' complained the devil. 'I can't move your cottage back –'

'I'd rather you didn't, anyway,' said Ellie. 'I like it here.'

'I suppose the simplest thing would be to provide a new pub.'

Just then George limped in, hungry and out of temper. But he couldn't help cheering up when he saw how beautifully Ellie had mended the carpet.

'I wish to give in my notice,' said the fox.

'Oh, very well,' growled George. 'You never did a hand's turn of work, anyway; I don't know why I kept you.'

'Goodbye, your Highness!' Ellie called, as the fox jumped out through the back window and ran off into the wood.

'Why did you call him that?' George said in surprise.

'Didn't you recognize him? It was Lucifer.'

'Well, I'll be –' said George, and went racing after the fox. But of course he was far too late.

'Anyway,' said Ellie, putting three plates of sizzling bubble-and-squeak on the table when George came hobbling back, 'after all he did teach you to mend things, you've got a craft for life.'

'That's the trouble,' said George.

But the bubble-and-squeak was so delicious that after supper he asked Ellie to marry him. Uncle Tom had gone off to the pub; they strolled along the village to find him and tell him their news.

Halfway along they found him sitting on the grass of the new roundabout, gazing up at the fountain.

'Why, Uncle Tom, whatever are you doing there?'

' 'Tis a fine new pub, can't you see, gal? I'm a-sitting in front of it drinking Audit Ale at one o' they little white iron occidental tables.'

Nothing they could say to him would persuade Uncle Tom that a new pub had not been built in the middle of the roundabout. The Prince of Darkness it was called, he said.

George and Ellie got married and she helped him with the mending, at which she soon became as skilful as he. With her help, he did not have to do more than a reasonable day's work; there was time to go skating in the winter and bluebell-picking in the spring. They all lived in Uncle Tom's cottage, which was the more comfortable, and kept the other one as a mending workshop.

The Ministry for the Environment never sent anyone to collect the twenty miles of rolled-up dual carriageway, though George had it mended and ready, so one Sunday George converted it all to a switchback track for the village children, which made him very popular.

Lucifer quite often sat over a drink with Mr Mudgwick in his invisible pub. And, as the fox, he would sometimes come and lie in front of Ellie's kitchen fire, after George had forgiven him. It took a while for George to swallow the fact that Lucifer had taught him to enjoy work, and that he'd have to do it for the rest of his life.

Two Tales of Burnt Porridge

FAR away from here lies a huge forest, as big as all the countries of Europe put together. It is full of wolves and bears and hyenas and wild boars and gnomes and trolls and even possibly a dragon or two; the trees in it are so immense that birds, leaving their nests to go out for a quick worm, sometimes become lost and take days to find their way home again.

Despite all the perils in the forest, it is a beautiful place; in springtime, when all the birds are singing together, their music is lovelier than that of the finest orchestra; even the mosquitos play overtures and suites of dances; the antlers of the stags that roam the glades are set with jewels, the fish swimming in the rocky streams are coloured like butterflies, and as for the butterflies themselves, they are so wonderful that it is no use trying to describe them. Also in this region are mountains with fiery hearts, caves full of mysteries, and two lost villages.

The forest is called Sloppy Chutney.

The villages, of course, are not lost so far as the people who live in them are concerned. *They* know where they are, all right, and are quite content to be there. But a traveller coming from outside the forest might travel for the whole of his life and never lay eyes on the church steeple of either place.

The villages are called Bad Whoopingcough (which lies to the east of the forest) and Burnt Porridge (which lies to the west) and there is a fierce feud between them; the people in Bad Whoopingcough think that the Burnt Porridge lot are a set of swindling no-goods; while the inhabitants of Burnt Porridge know that everyone in Bad

Whoopingcough is both lazy and stupid. Luckily it is very seldom that a native of one place meets a native of the other; the villages are so far apart that if you set off to travel between them, you would have to pass at least three birthdays on your walk through the forest and nobody in either place would wish to do *that*.

Both villages are very pretty; each has a little white church, an old timbered inn, a duck-pond, a circular green, a maypole in the middle, and a village shop selling everything that you could possibly want, so long as your requirements were reasonable. But the people in Burnt Porridge know that their village is by far the more beautiful, so I am going to tell you about it.

Although Burnt Porridge lies so remote in the forest, it is not an old-fashioned place; by no means. The inhabitants have every modern invention that the heart could wish for: TV, radio, electricity, natural gas; even the telephone. The three farmers, Farmer Broom, Farmer Leaves, and Farmer Iron, cultivate their fields and milk their cows with the very latest machinery; the village saint, St Withold, keeps his little cell in the church bell-tower warm by means of oil-fired heating; even the village witch, Mrs Murky, rides about on a vacuum cleaner.

The only two people in the village who don't bother about the progress of science are little Sam (who lives with his granny in the last house on the right) and his friend the Bumblebear (who lives in the forest just outside the village, but spends almost every day with little Sam). These two friends are happiest when they are wandering among the trees hand in hand, looking for nuts and wild honey, and beautiful orchids and gorgeously coloured feathers from the tails of the lyre-birds who make their nests in the towering ilex trees.

Well:

One day the village genius, Albert Einstein Shakespeare Smith, invented a new kind of sleigh. It was propelled by a condenser, which collected great bundles of energy from the sun's rays. Using this energy, the sleigh could be driven along at a very rapid speed; it was even possible, Mr Shakespeare Smith declared, that the sleigh might cross the forest to Bad Whoopingcough inside of a day.

'Who'd want to go *there*?' said Mrs Murky, the village witch, scornfully.

All the inhabitants of Burnt Porridge had assembled to admire the wonderful sleigh.

''Tis a fine commodious vehicle, to be sure,' said Farmer Iron.

'Bit top-heavy, look you,' said Farmer Leaves.

'Now isn't it a fine thing, we can all be setting off for a musical sleighride,' said Farmer Broom.

'Oh, please, do let's all go for a ride!' cried little Sam. 'Can the Bumblebear come too?'

'Xxxxxx,' said the Bumblebear, and rubbed his furry wings lovingly against the side of the sleigh.

Mr Shakespeare Smith did a bit of calculation and worked out that there would be nine cubic inches of space on the sleigh for each person in the village. So they all climbed on board except for Sam's granny, who said she saw no point in idle joyriding, she certainly did not want to go along if they were likely to get within sight of Bad Whoopingcough, if ever she were wishful to call on her sister Maria (and that sulky layabout husband of hers) she would make up her own mind; she'd stay at home and put on a kettle for tea, she daresaid they'd all be glad of a cup when they got back.

So all the rest of them piled on to the sleigh. They wrapped up warm, for it was wintertime, with bearskins and sheepskins and buskins and moleskins and wineskins and galligaskins; they took their musical instruments with them, crumhorns, shawms, sorduns, and rebecs. St Withold came along for the ride, and he brought his friend St Gothold, who was over on a visit from Bad Whoopingcough. So it was just as well that Sam's granny had decided to stay behind.

Mr Shakespeare Smith pressed the starter switch.

They had a little trouble before they got going; first the sleigh went down into the ground like a lift; then it went sideways. However after an hour or two these tendencies were corrected, and they took off at a great speed, whizzing through the snow-laden trees.

'Sure, 'tis an elegant conveyance,' said Farmer Broom.

'I'll be in Scotland afore ye,' said Farmer Iron.

'Bit bumpy, look you,' said Farmer Leaves.

Mrs Murky, the village witch, was carrying a spell over her arm, in case of any trouble or difficulty; but several times it was nearly jolted off, so at last she rolled it up and used it as a cushion.

Little Sam sat on the Bumblebear's lap.

To pass the time, they all played on their musical instruments and sang the village song:

> There's no place like Burnt Porridge
> However far you forage
> Even in outer space
> You won't find such a place
> Hooray for our town
> May nothing ever knock it down.

They made such a loud and joyful noise as they careered along that the birds rose from the branches with startled cries, and the deer went bounding away, their jewelled antlers sparkling like Christmas trees.

The snow was deep and firm; the sleigh went as fast as an express-train, and Shakespeare Smith steered it among the trees with wonderful skill.

Unfortunately the singing and playing of the passengers

woke from their winter sleep a pack of wolves, who yawned, stretched themselves, and began running along behind the sleigh, howling at the tops of their voices.

'Och, maircy, hark to the wanchancie beasts,' said Farmer Iron.

'In need of a square meal they sound to me,' said Farmer Leaves. 'Make for home again, maybe we had better?'

'Oh, I *did* hope we'd get to Bad Whoopingcough,' said little Sam.

'Xxxxxx,' said the Bumblebear.

So Mr Shakespeare Smith turned the sleigh towards home again.

But they had come a long distance by now, through the frozen forest; they had a long distance to go back again. Furthermore Mr Shakespeare Smith was having a little trouble with the magnet; the sun had gone behind a grey cloud and he wasn't getting much power.

The wolves began to overtake the sleigh.

'Saints presairve us, we shall all be swallowed whole,' said Farmer Broom.

'Cast a spell at the wolves, maybe you had better, Mrs M?' said Farmer Leaves.

So Mrs Murky fished out the spell from under her and cast it at the wolves. Unfortunately it got tangled up in the Bumblebear's whiskers and fell short; it was lost in the snow.

'Throw out some ballast we shall have to, I am thinking,' said Farmer Leaves.

' 'Tis the passengers we'll need to be consigning, for there's no ballast in it at all,' said Farmer Broom.

'Hoots, toots, who'd ha' thocht o' sich a contingency,' said Farmer Iron.

Little Sam was the smallest passenger, so they threw him out first, and the Bumblebear flew after him.

The smallest of the wolves jumped into the gap they had left on the sleigh.

'Murder!' said Farmer Broom, 'who'll we disburse next?'

Next they threw out Mrs Murky.

'A tough morsel they'll be finding her, I'm thinking,' said Farmer Leaves.

Another wolf jumped into the sleigh.

'Losh, there's no satisfying the sackless brutes,' said Farmer Iron.

So they threw out St Gothold. His halo caught on a twig, and he dangled there for several minutes before falling into the snow.

Another wolf jumped into the sleigh.

Then they tossed out St Withold. *He* sank into the snow right up to his ears; nothing could be seen of him but the halo.

One by one, all the inhabitants of Burnt Porridge were thrown out of the sleigh.

One by one, all the wolves in the pack jumped on board.

' 'Tis yourself we'll need to be relinquishing this time, Farmer Iron,' said Farmer Broom.

So they threw out Farmer Iron.

'Your turn it is, now, just, Farmer Broom,' said Farmer Leaves.

So they threw out Farmer Broom. Another wolf jumped on board; most of the wolves were in the sleigh by this time.

'Jump out myself, next, suppose I will have to,' said Farmer Leaves.

So he jumped out.

'Fine goings-on, when you have to give up your seat in a public conveyance to a pack of wolves who don't even pay rates; not what I am used to, no indeed!'

'Ah, sure, and isn't it right the poor beasts should have a bit of a diversion once in a way?' said Farmer Broom, as he ran behind.

So the wolves sat in the sleigh, playing on crumhorns, shawms, sorduns, and rebecs, while all the inhabitants of Burnt Porridge ran after it, howling at the tops of their voices.

The Bumblebear carried little Sam, however.

When they were about half a mile from home, and the setting sun was hidden altogether by thick, dark clouds, the magnet broke down entirely and the sleigh came to a stop. By now it was snowing quite hard. So they abandoned the sleigh in the forest, with all the wolves sitting on it, and walked the rest of the way home. The Bumblebear flew ahead, on his big furry wings, carrying little Sam; when these two reached the village they told Sam's granny that the others were close behind.

Sam's granny had a big pile of crumpets already toasted and buttered; the kettle was just on the boil.

'Maybe 'tis the way we should have invited the wolves in for a sup of tea?' said Farmer Broom, as they all sat round Sam's Granny's tea table. Little Sam was on the Bumblebear's lap, eating crumpets and strawberry jam.

'Eat us out of house and home they would, the ravening quadrupeds,' pointed out Farmer Leaves.

'Better pickle on a cracket trencher than muckle wi' a leesome wolf,' said Farmer Iron. 'Yon Bumblebear eats enough for two as it is.'

'Xxxxxx,' said the Bumblebear.

*

In the forest of Sloppy Chutney, spring is a wonderful time. The primroses and hellebores are so big and yellow and plentiful that the grassy ground seems sprinkled with stars; the birds sing so long and so loud that frequently they become quite tired out, and are to be found lying asleep on their backs under the ilex trees. New green leaves grow so thickly that walking through the forest is like pushing your way through a green featherbed.

One spring day little Sam and his friend the Bumble-bear were wandering along the glades, picking violets, anemones, and bluebells, and listening to the cuckoo. Little Sam was counting the calls.

'Two thousand, two hundred, and twenty-one,' he said.

'Cuckoo,' said the cuckoo.

'Two thousand, two hundred, and twenty-two,' said little Sam.

'Xxxxxx,' said the Bumblebear, rubbing some pollen off its furry wings.

In the village of Burnt Porridge, Albert Einstein Shakespeare Smith, the village genius, was building a skyscraper.

He had reached the hundred-and-fifth storey.

The three farmers, Farmer Broom, Farmer Leaves, and Farmer Iron, were leaning on their cultivators, and watching the progress of his work.

'Faith, 'tis a prestigious building,' said Farmer Broom, watching Smith clamber up the ladder with a bucket of bricks.

'No sense in it do I see at all,' said Farmer Leaves.

''Twill house the surplus population, amn't I after telling you?' said Farmer Broom.

'Surplus population?' said Farmer Iron, glancing up and down the empty street.

Meanwhile, far away in the forest, little Sam and the Bumblebear had found a burning mountain. Flames and bits of red-hot coal kept bursting out from its wide-open top; and sections of top kept breaking off and falling down inside the mountain; then they would be blown out again, like splashes from a boiling saucepan.

'Croopus,' said little Sam. 'The mountain's on fire.'

'Xxxxxx,' said the Bumblebear.

While they watched it, the mountain blew another huge section of itself up into the air.

'It's blown another bit of its top off,' said little Sam. 'Do you think we ought to tell somebody?'

'Xxxxxx,' said the Bumblebear.

They hurried back to the village, hand in hand.

'The mountain's blown its top off!' cried little Sam.

'Wasteful; untidy that is, but not much to do about it, I am thinking,' said Farmer Leaves.

'Better a dwining mountain than a brickle haggis,' said Farmer Iron.

Just then the mountain blew off another bit of its top. Even from the village this could be seen. Furthermore, pieces of burning mountain showered all over the green. Mrs Murky, the village witch, had just washed a lot of spells and hung them out on her clothesline; they were all singed by red-hot dust. Mrs Murky was annoyed. Sam's granny fetched a broom and began sweeping the cinders from the street, shaking her head disapprovingly.

'I'm scared!' said little Sam.

'Xxxxxx,' said the Bumblebear.

'Ah, sure, what harm? 'Tis only yon summit letting off steam, whatever,' said Farmer Broom.

'Summit to be said for that,' said Farmer Iron.

Little Sam shouted up to Mr Shakespeare Smith, on top of his skyscraper.

'Mr Smith, the mountain's on fire! Can't you do something about it? I'm scared!'

Mr Shakespeare Smith was becoming very worried about his skyscraper, which had developed a sideways tilt; he paid no attention to little Sam. He was trying to persuade the skyscraper to lean the other way, by dangling a bucket of bricks from the top. This did not help in the least.

At that moment another piece of burning mountain landed on Farmer Iron's hen-house. Luckily the hens were all out of doors, enjoying the spring sunshine, but they were very upset at the damage to their house.

'Losh, to be sure, yon mountain's unco wampish,' said Farmer Iron.

' 'Tis the spring that's in it,' said Farmer Broom.

'Oh, please, can't you stop it?' said little Sam.

'Bit of a problem that, choose how,' said Farmer Leaves.

'Saints presairve us, it'll have us destroyed entirely,' said Farmer Broom. 'Maybe if their Reverences were to lay on a blessing, 'twould allay its unruliness.'

Little Sam ran along to the belfry and woke up St Withold, the village saint. He pulled on his halo and came along to survey the situation; his friend St Gothold, from the neighbouring village of Bad Whoopingcough, happened to be staying with him at the time, so he came along too.

The two saints put a blessing on the mountain, but that didn't do any good. In fact another large piece of top blew off and fell on to Mrs Murky's cucumber patch. She was not pleased.

'Why don't you cast a spell?' said little Sam.

The trouble was that all Mrs Murky's spells had had holes burned in them.

'Better be digging away the mountain with a bulldozer, I am thinking?' said Farmer Leaves.

'My bulldozer has a puncture,' said Farmer Iron.

'Mine needs a wee drap of oil, for 'tis after seizing up with the rust that's in it,' said Farmer Broom.

Farmer Leaves had lent his bulldozer to Mrs Murky

who wanted to move her house (which was a teapot standing on one leg) to the other end of the village; unfortunately a spell had lodged between the bulldozer's jaws and jammed them.

Then the mountain blew off another piece of top. This one landed on the roof of an empty house, which fell down.

'Musha, musha, what'll we do at all?' said Farmer Broom.

'I dinna rightly ken,' said Farmer Iron.

'Pour on a drop of water, we might?' said Farmer Leaves.

'What from?' said Farmer Iron.

''Tis the way Mr Shakespeare Smith might be loaning us the borry of his bucket,' said Farmer Broom.

'Och, aye, that's a canny notion,' said Farmer Iron. 'Yon Bumblebear could fly over the top o' the declivity and pour the water into the hole.'

They borrowed Mr Shakespeare's bucket (which he dropped just at that moment, scattering bricks far and wide) and filled it at the village well.

The Bumblebear revved up its wings. The Bumblebear was so top-heavy that it always had difficulty with take-off; getting airborne took some time and patience.

Little Sam wasn't very happy about this plan.

'Suppose the mountain blows off another piece of top and hits the Bumblebear?' he said.

'Ah, sure, 'twill be a noble and gallant mishap in the performance of the creature's duty,' said Farmer Broom.

The Bumblebear wasn't worried. Loading it wasn't too easy, though. The Bumblebear hovered six feet above ground, and Farmer Leaves passed up the bucket of water, getting rather splashed.

However, when it was poured into the burning hole at the top of the mountain, one bucketful of water didn't seem to make a great deal of difference.

'Maybe another bucketful would do the trick,' said Farmer Iron.

'Perhaps 'twould be better to bulldoze the mountain, after all,' said Farmer Broom. 'I'll be giving my bulldozer a dram of oil.'

He fetched a can of oil from his cottage and poured it into the bulldozer. But just as he finished, the mountain blew off another section of top, which hit the bulldozer and flattened it.

'Glory be, and isn't that a sorrowful waste of oil?' said Farmer Broom.

'Xxxxxx,' said the Bumblebear, spilling a bucketful of water which little Sam had just handed up to it.

'In my opinion our village is doomed, look you,' said Farmer Leaves.

'Wae's me, 'tis an orra clamjamfry,' said Farmer Iron.

In their agitation over the burning mountain, everyone had forgotten Mr Shakespeare Smith and his skyscraper, which was tilting farther and farther, like a melting candle.

Just at that moment it toppled over entirely and fell right into the crater at the top of the mountain, plugging the hole and putting out the fire inside.

'Will ye be after looking at that, then!' said Farmer Broom. 'Now where'll we be housing the surplus population?'

'Poor bit of foundation-laying that was, indeed to goodness,' said Farmer Leaves.

'Eh, well. Better a mawkin's wanion than kittle breakfast wi' a wallydraigle,' said Farmer Iron.

Everybody went in to tea, except for Albert Einstein Shakespeare Smith, who was thinking.

Then little Sam and the Bumblebear wandered back into the forest, to pick some more primroses and hellebores, which grew scattered over the grassy ground, thick as stars.

Humblepuppy

Our house was furnished mainly from auction sales. When you buy furniture that way you get a lot of extra things besides the particular piece that you were after, since the stuff is sold in lots: Lot 13, two Persian rugs, a set of golf-clubs, a sewing-machine, a walnut radio-cabinet, and a plinth.

It was in this way that I acquired a tin deedbox, which came with two coal-scuttles and a broom cupboard. The deedbox is solid metal, painted black, big as a medium-sized suitcase. When I first brought it home I put it in my study, planning to use it as a kind of filing-cabinet for old typescripts. I had gone into the kitchen, and was busy arranging the brooms in their new home, when I heard a loud thumping coming from the direction of the study.

I went back, thinking that a bird must have flown through the window; no bird, but the banging seemed to be inside the deedbox. I had already opened it as soon as it was in my possession, to see if there were any diamonds or bearer bonds worth thousands of pounds inside (there weren't), but I opened it again. The key was attached to the handle by a thin chain. There was nothing inside. I shut it. The banging started again. I opened it.

Still nothing inside.

Well, this was broad daylight, two o'clock on Thursday afternoon, people going past in the road outside and a radio schools programme chatting away to itself in the next room. It was not a ghostly kind of time, so I put my hand into the empty box and moved it about.

Something shrank away from my hand. I heard a faint,

scared whimper. It could almost have been my own, but wasn't. Knowing that someone – something? – else was afraid too put heart into me. Exploring carefully and gently around the interior of the box I felt the contour of a small, bony, warm, trembling body with big awkward feet, and silky dangling ears, and a cold nose that, when I found it, nudged for a moment anxiously but trustingly into the palm of my hand. So I knelt down, put the other hand into the box as well, cupped them under a thin little ribby chest, and lifted out Humblepuppy.

He was quite light.

I couldn't see him, but I could hear his faint inquiring whimper, and I could hear his toenails scratch on the floorboards.

Just at that moment the cat, Taffy, came in.

Taffy has a lot of character. Every cat has a lot of character, but Taffy has more than most, all of it inconvenient. For instance, although he is very sociable, and longs for company, he just despises company in the form of dogs. The mere sound of a dog barking two streets away is enough to make his fur stand up like a porcupine's quills and his tail swell like a mushroom cloud.

Which it did the instant he saw Humblepuppy.

Now here is the interesting thing. I could feel and hear Humblepuppy, but couldn't see him; Taffy, apparently, could see and smell him, but couldn't feel him. We soon discovered this. For Taffy, sinking into a low, gladiator's crouch, letting out all the time a fearsome throaty wauling like a bagpipe revving up its drone, inched his way along to where Humblepuppy huddled trembling by my left foot, and then dealt him what ought to have been a swinging right-handed clip on the ear. 'Get out of my house, you filthy little canine scum!' was what he was plainly intending to convey.

But the swipe failed to connect; instead it landed on my shin. I've never seen a cat so astonished. It was like watching a kitten meet itself for the first time in a looking-glass. Taffy ran round to the back of where Humblepuppy was sitting; felt; smelt; poked gingerly with a paw; leapt back nervously; crept forward again. All the time Humblepuppy just sat, trembling a little, giving out this faint beseeching sound that meant: 'I'm only a poor little mongrel without a smidgeon of harm in me. *Please* don't do anything nasty! I don't even know how I came here.'

It certainly was a puzzle how he had come. I rang the auctioneers (after shutting Taffy *out* and Humblepuppy *in* to the study with a bowl of water and a handful of Boniebisk, Taffy's favourite breakfast food).

The auctioneers told me that Lot 12, Deedbox, coal-scuttles and broom cupboard, had come from Riverland Rectory, where Mr Smythe, the old rector, had lately died aged ninety. Had he ever possessed a dog, or a puppy? They couldn't say; they had merely received instructions from a firm of lawyers to sell the furniture.

I never did discover how poor little Humblepuppy's ghost got into that deedbox. Maybe he was shut in by mistake, long ago, and suffocated; maybe some callous Victorian gardener dropped him, box and all, into a river, and the box was later found and fished out.

Anyway, and whatever had happened in the past, now that Humblepuppy had come out of his box, he was very pleased with the turn his affairs had taken, ready to be grateful and affectionate. As I sat typing I'd often hear a patter-patter, and feel his small chin fit itself comfortably over my foot, ears dangling. Goodness knows what kind of a mixture he was; something between a spaniel and a terrier, I'd guess. In the evening, watching television or sitting by the fire, one would suddenly find his warm weight leaning against one's leg. (He didn't put on a lot of weight while he was with us, but his bony little ribs filled out a bit.)

For the first few weeks we had a lot of trouble with Taffy, who was very surly over the whole business and blamed me bitterly for not getting rid of this low-class intruder. But Humblepuppy was extremely placating, got back into his deedbox whenever the atmosphere became too volcanic, and did his very best not to be a nuisance.

By and by Taffy thawed. As I've said, he is really a very sociable cat. Although quite old, seventy cat years, he dearly likes cheerful company, and generally has some young cat friend who comes to play with him, either in the house or the garden. In the last few years we've had Whisky, the black-and-white pub cat, who used to sit washing the smell of fish-and-chips off his fur under the dripping tap in our kitchen sink; Tetanus, the hairdresser's thickset black, who took a fancy to sleep on top of our china-cupboard every night all one winter, and used to startle me very much by jumping down heavily on to my shoulder as I made the breakfast coffee; Sweet Charity, a little grey Persian who came to a sad end under the wheels of a police-car; Charity's grey-and-white stripey cousin Fred, whose owners presently moved from next door to another part of the town.

It was soon after Fred's departure that Humblepuppy arrived, and from my point of view he couldn't have been more welcome. Taffy missed Fred badly, and expected *me* to play with him instead; it was sad to see this large elderly tabby rushing hopefully up and down the stairs after breakfast, or hiding behind the armchair and jumping out on to nobody; or howling, howling, howling at me until I escorted him out into the garden, where he'd rush to the lavender-bush which had been the traditional hiding-place of Whisky, Tetanus, Charity, and Fred in succession. Cats have their habits and histories, just the same as humans.

So sometimes, on a working morning, I'd be at my wits' end, almost on the point of going across the town to our ex-neighbours, ringing their bell, and saying, 'Please can Fred come and play?' Specially on a rainy, uninviting day when Taffy was pacing gloomily about the house with drooping head and switching tail, grumbling about the weather and the lack of company, and blaming me for both.

Humblepuppy's arrival changed all that.

At first Taffy considered it necessary to police him, and that kept him fully occupied for hours. He'd sit on guard by the deedbox till Humblepuppy woke up in the morning, and then he'd follow officiously all over the house, wherever the visitor went. Humblepuppy was slow and cautious in his explorations, but by degrees he picked up courage and found his way into every corner. He never once made a puddle; he learned to use Taffy's cat-flap and go out into the garden, though he was always more timid outside and would scamper for home at any loud noise. Planes and cars terrified him, he never became used to them; which made me still more certain that he had been in that deedbox for a long, long time, since before such things were invented.

Presently he learned, or Taffy taught him, to hide in the lavender-bush like Whisky, Charity, Tetanus, and Fred; and the two of them used to play their own ghostly version of touch-last for hours on end while I got on with my typing.

When visitors came, Humblepuppy always retired to his deedbox; he was decidedly scared of strangers; which made his behaviour with Mr Manningham, the new rector of Riverland, all the more surprising.

I was dying to learn anything I could of the old rectory's history, so I'd invited Mr Manningham to tea.

He was a thin, gentle, quiet man, who had done missionary work in the Far East and fell ill and had to come back to England. He seemed a little sad and lonely; said he still missed his Far East friends and work. I liked him. He told me that for a large part of the nineteenth century the Riverland living had belonged to a parson called Swannett, the Reverend Timothy Swannett, who lived to a great age and had ten children.

'He was a great-uncle of mine, as a matter of fact. But why do you want to know all this?' Mr Manningham asked. His long thin arm hung over the side of his chair; absently he moved his hand sideways and remarked, 'I didn't notice that you had a puppy.' Then he looked down and said, 'Oh!'

'He's never come out for a stranger before,' I said.

Taffy, who maintains a civil reserve with visitors, sat motionless on the nightstore heater, eyes slitted, sphinx-like.

Humblepuppy climbed invisibly on to Mr Manningham's lap.

We agreed that the new rector probably carried a familiar smell of his rectory with him; or possibly he reminded Humblepuppy of his great-uncle, the Rev. Swannett.

Anyway, after that, Humblepuppy always came scampering joyfully out if Mr Manningham dropped in to tea, so of course I thought of the rector when summer holiday time came round.

During the summer holidays we lend our house and cat to a lady publisher and her mother who are devoted to cats and think it a privilege to look after Taffy and spoil him. He is always amazingly overweight when we get back. But the old lady has an allergy to dogs, and is frightened of them too; it was plainly out of the question

that she should be expected to share her summer holiday
with the ghost of a puppy.

So I asked Mr Manningham if he'd be prepared to take
Humblepuppy as a boarder, since it didn't seem a case for
the usual kind of boarding-kennels; he said he'd be
delighted.

I drove Humblepuppy out to Riverland in his deedbox;
he was rather miserable on the drive, but luckily it is not
far. Mr Manningham came out into the garden to meet us.
We put the box down on the lawn and opened it.

I've never heard a puppy so wildly excited. Often I'd
been sorry that I couldn't see Humblepuppy, but I was
never sorrier than on that afternoon, as we heard him
rushing from tree to familiar tree, barking joyously,
dashing through the orchard grass – you could see it
divide as he whizzed along – coming back to bounce up
against us, all damp and earthy and smelling of leaves.

'He's going to be happy with you, all right,' I said, and
Mr Manningham's grey, lined face crinkled into its
thoughtful smile as he said, 'It's the place more than me,
I think.'

Well, it was both of them, really.

After the holiday, I went to collect Humblepuppy,
leaving Taffy haughty and standoffish, sniffing our cases.
It always takes him a long time to forgive us for going
away.

Mr Manningham had a bit of a cold and was sitting by
the fire in his study, wrapped in a shetland rug. Humblepuppy was on his knee. I could hear the little dog's tail
thump against the arm of the chair when I walked in, but
he didn't get down to greet me. He stayed in Mr Manningham's lap.

'So you've come to take back my boarder,' Mr Manningham said.

There was nothing in the least strained about his voice or smile but – I just hadn't the heart to take back Humble-puppy. I put my hand down, found his soft wrinkly forehead, rumpled it a bit, and said,

'Well – I was sort of wondering: our spoilt old cat seems to have got used to being on his own again; I was wondering whether – by any chance – you'd feel like keeping him?'

Mr Manningham's face lit up. He didn't speak for a minute; then he put a gentle hand down to find the small head, and rubbed a finger along Humblepuppy's chin.

'Well,' he said. He cleared his throat. 'Of course, if you're *quite* sure –'

'Quite sure.' My throat needed clearing too.

'I hope you won't catch my cold,' Mr Manningham said. I shook my head and said, 'I'll drop in to see if you're better in a day or two,' and went off and left them together.

Poor Taffy was pretty glum over the loss of his play-mate for several weeks; we had two hours' purgatory every morning after breakfast while he hunted for Humblepuppy high and low. But gradually the memory faded and, thank goodness, now he has found a new friend, Little Grey Furry, a nephew, cousin or other relative of Charity and Fred. Little Grey Furry has learned to play hide-and-seek in the lavender-bush, and to use our cat-flap, and clean up whatever's in Taffy's food bowl, so all is well in that department.

But I still miss Humblepuppy. I miss his cold nose exploring the palm of my hand, as I sit thinking, in the middle of a page, and his warm weight leaning against my knee as he watches the commercials. And the scritch-scratch of his toenails on the dining-room floor and the flump, flump, as he comes downstairs, and the small hollow in a cushion as he settles down with a sigh.

Oh well. I'll get over it, just as Taffy has. But I was wondering about putting an ad. into *Our Dogs* or *Pets' Monthly*: Wanted, ghost of mongrel puppy. Warm welcome, loving home. Any reasonable price paid.

It might be worth a try.

The River Boy

THE river curled about in the narrow valley, dipping and plunging from rock to rock in miniature cascades, here sliding in deceptive silence over a flat shelf, there chuckling and whispering across a bed of pebbles.

Knee-deep in its coolness the boy strolled and stooped, selecting round, polished stones for his sling. They glittered an instant as he picked them out, drops flying from his fingers; then they dried in the fierce afternoon heat. The swift-running water arched against his legs, and when he skipped a rejected stone across the river it whirled downstream with the current.

A pouch in his leather kilt held the stones that he considered suitable; he wore no other clothes and his skin was tanned by the sun to the identical pale brown of his hair so that on his neck it would have been impossible to tell where skin ended and hair began, save that the skin had a young, matt surface whereas the hair, from constant bleaching, wore a sort of silvery nimbus.

Presently the pouch was full and the boy made his way ashore, jumping from rock to rock, balancing himself with prehensile toes and outspread arms. The river ran between low, rocky walls; above them the short grass sloped in a smooth, cuplike curve to the cliffs and formed the sides of the valley, which was only a few yards wide. It was treeless; but ferns, heath, and berry bushes grew everywhere out of cracks in the rock, and the ground was covered with thyme, rockrose, and saxifrage. The boy flung himself down on this scented carpet and began to eat a piece of flat dough-cake, and to pull berries off the nearest bush.

Grasshoppers sang in the heat; there was no other sound.

When he had finished his meal he lay on his stomach, trailing a berry at the end of a long stem of grass over the surface of the water. But the day was too bright to catch any fish; they were all hanging in the wavering shadows of the rocks, or down against the mossed slopes of the waterfalls or hidden in clefts. And after a while the boy's head sank lower on his arms and he slept, while the sun moved over the sky and the shadows of the western cliff slowly began to lengthen across the valley.

After a couple of hours he began to stir, and suddenly he sat bolt upright with a look of disquiet.

There seemed nothing to cause alarm; the valley drowsed, golden and peaceful in the warm evening; only far overhead a couple of kites wheeled about the empty sky. The boy lay down again with his ear to the ground and his hands clasped over his head. His eyes narrowed as he heard a faraway thrumming like the patter of rain on oiled silk. It was the sound of hoofs.

He jumped up, went to the cliff-face, and began climbing it. He did not seem to hurry, but his ascent was swift; he gripped a ledge with his toes, thrust his fist into a vertical crack, clenched it, and almost ran up the sheer wall like a fly on a window-pane. Standing on a huge, flat-iron-shaped rock at the top he gazed round, shading his eyes with both hands.

From this height the whole length of his little valley could easily be seen. It was no more than a crack in the land that spread in all directions as far as the eye travelled; a blond, rolling, upland country, now bleached pale brown by the savage midsummer sun. Nothing grew up there but the long, fine grass; and the rolling lines of the hills were broken only by sand-coloured rocks scattered here and there as if they had been dropped by giants. All around rose the far, blue, jagged peaks of mountains which, in the dry air, looked close at hand; but they were three days' journey away.

After he had watched a short while, the boy tensed, as a tiny black patch no bigger than his hand appeared for a moment or two sliding over one of the straw-coloured ridges, and then sank from sight behind another.

With a look of indecision he walked the few hundred yards along the cliff-edge to the lower end of the valley. Here the river, in the abrupt manner peculiar to limestone streams, plunged underground and vanished just before it reached what had once been a waterfall but was now a dry cleft in a precipice. Far below the deserted watercourse began again and ran away down a bleached and barren valley for ten miles. At the lower end of this the tree-line started. There were a few dwarf rowans and ashes, and behind them lay a village.

It was called Pué, and the boy knew it well; he had lived there until when he was eight his father had been stoned to death as a wizard and he had been driven out as a witch's brat to fend for himself in the dry uplands, which the villagers called the ter' sec'. He would probably have starved to death if he had not discovered the hidden valley. Nobody from below ever came up here.

He wondered what sort of reception he would get if he went down with his news. Bad, probably. He had not been back by day for ten years, though he made occasional night raids to steal flour and oil. Presently, having decided against going down he turned back the way he had come. If the menace to his valley was to be averted, he must do the job himself.

It was a real enough menace. The black cloud on the horizon was one of the herds of fierce little black mountain bulls which range at will over the uplands. In the spring the villagers catch and corral the heifers and calves, but the bulls are considered useless and are left to go free. Generally they stay on the western slopes of the mountains where the moisture-laden winds from the sea keep the grass fresh and long during the summer months, but this had been an exceptionally dry season and they must have been driven by hunger far from their usual haunts. The boy knew that if they came much farther they would soon scent the water in his little slip of an oasis, and once they came piling into it down the track at the upper end it would be completely devastated.

The herd might easily hold a hundred or more. His berry bushes, with their load of fruit, which he had intended to dry for winter, and his patches of root vegetables and grain would be reduced to muddy pulp by their countless needle-sharp hoofs; the stream would be fouled and the fish trampled and killed.

He glanced at the horizon again. It would be several hours before they arrived, and he let himself down the valley-wall again and went to work methodically, stowing away what he could; the strips of goats' meat and fish that he had spread out to dry on flat rocks were placed in his cave halfway up the rock face, together with a few early ears of grain.

He considered his bees in their woven grass skep, but they were still actively humming about collecting nectar from the heath and rockrose, and he did not dare risk moving them; they would have to take their chance. Luckily he had already collected some of that season's honey and stored it in clay boxes at the back of the cave.

He stacked away his grass fishing nets and few stone tools, wondered if it would be worth digging up some of the roots and decided not to; they were not yet ripe and would only go rotten unless they were left in the ground until the frosts came.

All this had taken time; the sun had left the sky, which

turned first green, then a deep tender blue with the
pricking of a few stars. It was cold up here at night.
Normally if he were going to be out after dark he put on a
leather jerkin, but his present plan made that pointless.

He climbed up to the head of the valley where a steep
zigzag track – the path the bulls would come down – led
up to the plateau. There was a roar of water, for here the
river burst from a hole in the cliff and cataracted down
into the valley. By day it was a splendid sight, a clear
green torrent of limestone water springing out of the
whitish rock, but now there was nothing to be seen save a
pale glimmer reflecting the early stars.

Presently the moon rose, and the boy was glad of it,
for the waterfall drowned any other sound and he was uncertain how close the cattle had come. He went up to the
top of the track and stared intently over the pale, rolling
landscape. A moving darkness caught his eye; there they
were, less than a mile off, coming along fast.

He ran down the path again, turned aside and plunged
into the stream, ducking directly under the heart of the
waterfall which now, under the moon, had become a spout
of silver falling into a pool of curdled light.

There was room to stand behind the fall and it made a
good hiding-place, drowning sound and smell. He knew
that if the bulls caught wind of him too soon it would
ruin his hopes, for they were wildly fierce, and the mere
whiff of a human would send them stampeding up and
down the valley; if he found himself in the path of such a
stampede his life would not be worth the snap of a
twig.

His kilt soon became soaked but he kept it on because of
the pouch holding his sling and stones, and the tiny knife,
the only one he possessed, tied by a thong to his waist-
band. Wound round his wrist and dangling in a coil was
the lariat, a strong slender buckskin rope that he used for

catching goats, and for dragging heavy loads up the cliff-face to his cave.

The wait seemed long but it was probably not more than ten or fifteen minutes; then suddenly and, as it seemed, silently the pool below the fall was filled with wedge-shaped, black bodies flicking tails and tossing horns as the bulls drank and drank after their long parching run over the waterless country.

The boy stood with every muscle tight, waiting for them to move. He knew that until they had drunk deep nothing short of a landslide would shift them, and he studied them through the sheets of spray, trying to decide which was the leader.

Finally a bull, slightly larger than the rest, began to nudge his way, swinging his head, towards the near bank.

Quick as a flash the boy left his cover and ducked through the pool, keeping low in the water to minimize his scent. When he reached the large bull he flung his noose over the great triangular head and jerked tight, then vaulted on its back. Leaning forward he grabbed the wide, curving horns and wrenched them round to turn the bull's head back up the cliff path.

With a frantic bellow the astonished bull started forward and the boy was almost unseated; he dug his knees into the bony shoulders and pressed his feet against the bull's flank. The animal lurched out of the water on to the bank, and then bolted up the track, furiously shaking his head from side to side in an effort to dislodge this alien thing from his back.

The rest of the herd followed, snorting, rearing, lashing out wickedly with their horns. The boy was thankful for his short start and for the narrowness of the path which prevented their coming alongside; he wondered what would happen when they reached the top. On the steep track it was difficult not to slide back down the knobby

ridge of the bull's spine, and as he did not want to check
its pace by dragging on the horns he lay at full length
pressing his bare feet tightly against its sides and gripping
with every muscle in his body. He felt the sling-stones
jerk out of his pouch but could not spare a hand to stop
them.

When they were halfway up, a further commotion
broke out in the herd behind, but he could not turn his
head far enough to see what was frightening them. They
pressed up close and he could feel their animal warmth
and steamy breath on his legs.

As the big bull staggered over the ridge at the top of the
cliff the boy was ready, and jabbed swiftly twice with his
knife into the rolling muscles above the shoulder, driving
the animal to frenzy. Then, leaning far forward, he bit the
bull's ear, sinking his teeth savagely through the fur to
the skin. The bull threw himself into an earth-shaking
trot, but he had paused for a moment and the herd had
caught up and were milling about him.

The boy felt a sickening pain in his knee as a chance-
tossed horn caught him and ripped flesh and muscle.
Ducking his head he stabbed again with the knife and the
goaded leader broke away from the others and pounded
off across open country, the herd following him in a
ragged, uneven line.

The boy shook himself into a more comfortable sitting
position, wincing with the pain of his hurt leg, and then
turned his head to see if most of the herd seemed to be
behind. He thought they were, and was filled with satisfaction.

The first part of his plan had gone well; now it only
remained to urge them far enough from the valley so that
they would not be tempted to go back, and then somehow
to separate the leader from the rest of the herd and escape
from his savage mount. It would be difficult, handicapped

as he was by his injured leg, but there was no sense in worrying about that yet; first he must get them several hours' run from the scent of grass and water.

The shaking of his body and the thunder of hoofs in his ears almost deafened him, but it seemed to him that there was still trouble in the herd behind. Looking back he saw the cause. A pair of luminous eyes glared greenly in his direction, very different from the shining, little, piglike, red eyes of the bulls, and he realized that a puma or prairie-lion must have leapt on to the back of one of the bulls while they were climing out of the valley – dropped from a rock above, very likely, and was now being carried along like himself, hanging with razor-sharp claws on the back of its terrified steed and intending to run the bull to death and then devour it.

Probably it had been shadowing the herd for days, waiting for an opportunity to get near.

The boy felt uneasy at this ferocious company, but there was nothing he could do about it, and very likely the puma would not trouble to attack him as long as it was satisfied with its present prey. He hoped that he would soon be able to break away from the main herd and leave the puma with them.

They galloped for a couple of hours, and the boy grew numb and tired from the heavy, shaking motion; all his bones felt stiff and bruised in their sockets, and his heavy, wet kilt hung round him in clammy folds. The night air of the ter' sec' was keen and dry, and his wound ached with cold. In spite of this his head several times dropped forward over the bull's neck and he recovered himself from sleep with an apprehensive jerk.

Night wore on, the sky began to pale. Presently the sun shot out of the eastern mountains, flaming rose and orange, for a short while dyeing the pale hills a strange, brilliant brick-red. Rousing himself the boy craned about

to see if he recognized the country they were passing through, but it was beyond his farthest boundaries.

They had run down a great slope, crossed countless dry gullies, and were now inching across an endless expanse of the bleached, parched mesa. The boy shook himself wider awake and noticed with relief that most of the herd were drawing away westwards. Looping the lariat firmly over his bull's left horn he kept up a persistent, gentle tug to head him always to the east, and saw with satisfaction that the gap was widening between the herd and himself.

With one exception.

Pounding along to the east of them was another solitary bull which sometimes came between them and the rising sun, throwing a long, fantastic shadow over the sandy ground. The boy screwed up his eyes and squinted into the light, wondering why the other bull was such an odd shape: it seemed humped or deformed in some way. Then the truth struck him; it was the bull that was being ridden to death by the puma.

With heels, knife, and teeth the boy urged his mount into a staggering gallop, hoping to out-distance this complication, but the other bull came heavily after them, and now the boy could see the puma distinctly, crouched, with its eyes glaring and claws buried deep in the black hide.

It became a horrible race. The boy's bull scented the puma and, uttering a bellow like the shriek of a saw, plunged on in a thudding, rolling gallop that seemed as if it would shake loose every bone in the boy's harassed body, but the other bull, desperate for companionship in its terror, managed to keep up with them. It was losing blood from several wounds and was frothing heavily; the boy began to hope that its strength would soon fail when, looking ahead, he saw a sight that made his heart sink.

In their frantic stampede the bulls had run straight against one of these strange limestone formations called *empedes*, which stretch for miles and are like a pavement of flat rocks; but a pavement made for giants, with paving-stones four or five feet across, and narrow gullies two or three feet wide between them. The spaces between the rocks are filled with fern, heath, and shrub, and the whole expanse looks as pretty as a rock-garden, but the boy felt despair as he saw it, and he tried in vain to wrench his bull round.

Now he understood why the rest of the herd had sheered off to the west; the wild cattle always avoid these *empedes* for, once among the rocks, they find it almost impossible to find a way out again and often become jammed in a narrowing crack and end up as a feast for the kites.

The boy's bull snorted and turned sideways but it was too late; they were already among the first rocks. He tried to steer his mount through the wider passages that would take them round and out of this terrible maze of stone, but it was hopeless; the bull panicked and plunged reck-lessly. The boy had to draw his feet up out of danger, for the edges of the rocks were as square and sharp as if they had been cut by the stonemason's trowel.

In a few minutes they were completely wedged in a tiny gully. Its sides were no more than three feet high and the trapped bull looked absurdly as if his legs had been sawn off, as he stood there snorting and rolling his eyes, unable to turn and incapable of going backwards.

Not ten yards away there was a savage bellowing and snarling. The second bull had been likewise brought to a standstill.

The boy stood up, staggering as he tried to put his weight on the injured leg. It had stiffened during the long, cold night and he could hardly get his foot to the ground. A fierce pain shot up his leg and the blood began flowing again. He set his teeth and took a few more steps, experimentally; then he heard a threatening growl and, looking up, saw that the puma had left its meal and was moving in his direction.

His heart sank. He had hoped that he might get away while it fed, but he saw that was impossible. It would leave the bull to follow the new, moving prey, and with his hurt leg he could not possibly command enough speed to get away.

He sprang back to his own bull and flung himself alongside its back, keeping within the protection of its horns. No puma will attack a bull in the open, for the sweep of the horns can open it from chest to tail. As long as the bull lived and the boy could keep awake he was reasonably safe.

With a disappointed snarl the puma returned to its abandoned meal, but after a time curiosity and the hunting instinct came over it once more and it slunk back for another survey, prowling cautiously just out of reach, its head low, its eyes blazing and full of menace. The imprisoned bull flung its head furiously from side to side and bellowed terror and defiance. The boy shouted and let the sunlight flash along the blade of his knife. Presently the puma moved away to a little distance and sank down, its head on its paws, dozing. Once or twice the boy tried to creep away when it seemed to be sleeping, but each time it sprang up and he had to run awkwardly back to the bull.

He began to despair, as the long, blisteringly hot day dragged on. He was faint and feverish from pain and hunger, and the bull's head was beginning to sag and its eyes to glaze; whereas the puma, fresh from its kill, fed and rested, was bright, fierce, and threatening. A couple of kites drifted down and began gorging on the second bull's carcase and the boy wondered uneasily how long it would be before they were picking *his* bones.

The puma hissed threateningly at the kites and they sheered off a hundred yards and dropped like plummets between the rocks.

Suddenly the boy had a wild flicker of hope. Could there possibly be a pot-hole there in the rock? He had come across a few such holes in his explorations – deep, dark chimneys that went down hundreds of feet to underground springs. The kites flew down to drink at these hidden waters, where no other living things could reach, and he had marvelled at their power to drop like stones and rise again almost vertically.

If there was a pot-hole there he had a chance – a faint, unlikely one – of outwitting the puma. It was worth trying, anyway; better than the slow fight against exhaustion and thirst, with the final grisly death when he was too weak to defend himself.

He lay still, gathering up his strength; chewing dry, straw-like grass in an effort to lessen the torturing thirst. Then, cautiously, he stood up, loosened the lariat from the bull's horns and re-coiled it, and began to move slowly towards the spot where the kites had dropped.

Instantly the puma was on the alert and began to creep in his direction with its tail switching.

The boy inched his way backwards, hardly taking his eyes from those of the cat, feeling his way with his toes, sweating at the pain of his wounded leg. All his instincts were crying out to run, but he knew that one rapid movement would bring the puma down on him; his only hope was to go slowly. He was terrified that he would stumble into one of the deep traps between the rocks, and every now and then he risked a glance behind for a second.

After ten minutes of this infinitesimally slow progress the boy took a chance; he picked up a fragment of rock and tossed it backwards over his shoulder. He heard it strike with a hollow echo and tinkle, and one of the kites flew up, croaking harshly and flapping its wings.

The puma paused, blinking, uncertain, and the boy's heart rose.

So there *was* a hole there.

Abandoning caution he turned and ran as fast as his leg would allow. A black gap yawned in front of him and he swung to the left and circled it, turning in time to see the puma come loping after him.

Now!

The lariat flashed snake-like across the mouth of the hole. Swift and true it noosed the puma's head, and with all his strength, the boy jerked it, flinging himself backwards. The puma, yowling rage and alarm, braced itself on the lip of the hole for a second, and then disappeared twisting into the blackness below, its plunging weight dragging the rope from the boy's bleeding wrist.

There was no sound from the hole; not the faintest splash or thud came back, and the boy, craning his neck over the edge, could see nothing but dark. The shaft looked as if it went down to infinity.

For a moment he reeled, giddy and sick. The swimming depth seemed ready to draw him down. He had just enough strength to turn and throw himself sideways into a deep, mossy crack between two rocks before he fainted.

*

When he came to himself it was evening. He felt chilly, bruised and stiff, but the fever had left him. He chewed a few berries and then limped back towards the bull, knowing that by himself, with his hurt leg, he would never be able to achieve the long, long trek back to his own valley.

Was the bull still alive? Its head had dropped forward

on to a patch of shrub, but as he came nearer it sprang up
with a snort and glared at him in panic.

He would have to be gentle, very gentle. Luckily the
bull was exhausted and bewildered by its long cramping
imprisonment in the full sun. He began speaking to it
soothingly, and holding its eyes with his, he caught hold
of the great horns and began to force it steadily backwards, checking the panicky swing of its head, never
ceasing his soothing flow of talk.

Slowly, slowly, one step at a time, the bull backed along
the narrow crevice until at last they came out on to open
ground and the boy, snatching his opportunity before the
bull realized its freedom, leapt once more on the broad,
bony back.

There was no fight left in the bull, and no speed either.
He ambled stiffly along at a slow walk, but the boy was
content with that. They were, at least, going in the right
direction. He spread himself along the bull's back in as
comfortable a position as he could achieve.

The evening was silent. The rest of the herd had long
since vanished into the foothills and nothing else was
moving on the wide upland. They breasted ridge after
ridge, and gradually the air freshened and the stars began
to prick out overhead.

Humming a tuneless song the boy turned his bull's
head towards one star, especially large and bright, which
gleamed and beckoned ahead and to the north.

The Gift Pig

ONCE there was a king whose queen, having just presented him with a baby princess, unfortunately died. The king was very upset at this, naturally. But he had to go on with the arrangements for the christening just the same, as court etiquette was strict on this point. What with his grief and distraction, however, and the yells of his daughter, an exceedingly lively and loud-voiced infant, the invitations to the christening were sent out in a very haphazard manner, and by mistake two elderly fairies were invited who were well known to loathe one another, so that when they met there was bound to be trouble, though when encountered separately they were pleasant enough.

The day of the christening arrived and at first all went well. The baby princess was christened Henrietta and behaved properly at the ceremony, crying a little but not too much. Then the whole party of relatives and guests strolled back from the royal chapel to the throne room where the reception was being held; the king noticed with alarm that the two elderly fairies were walking side by side. They seemed to be nodding in the most friendly way, but when he edged nearer to them he heard one say,

'How very well you are looking, darling Grizel! One wouldn't – by artificial light – take you for a day over two hundred.'

'Hardly surprising since I celebrated my hundred-and-eightieth birthday last week. But how are *you*, dear Bella? Do you think it was wise to attend the service in that draughty chapel? You walk with such a limp these days.'

'I am perfectly well, thank you, my love. And one does have one's social duty.'

'Especially when there is a free meal attached to it, tee hee!'

'But I confess I hardly expected to see you here – I understood the king's friends were all intelligent and – well, you know – *creative* people.'

'Creative, my angel? In that case, do tell me how *you* qualify for admission?'

Shuddering, the poor king made haste to cut the cake and circulate the sherry in hopes of sweetening these acid ladies. He wished that he could get rid of them before the visitors began to give their christening presents, but saw no way to.

Presently the guests, fairy and otherwise, having eaten every crumb of cake and drunk all the sherry, began depositing their gifts and taking their leave. The baby, pink and good in her cradle, was given whole rooms full of silver and coral rattles, shoals of shawls, bonnets and bootees by the bushel, mounds of matinee jackets and mittens, stacks of embroidered smocks and knitted socks. Besides this, she was endowed with good health, a friendly and cheerful nature, intelligence, and a logical mind.

Then the fairy Bella stepped forward and, smiling at the king, said,

'You must forgive me if my wish is not quite so pleasant as some of the preceding ones, but meeting – ahem – such very *odd* company in your palace has made me nervous and brought on a migraine. Let the princess rue the day that someone gives her a pig, for if ever that happens she will turn into a pig herself.'

'Moreover,' said the fairy Grizel, coming to the other side of the cradle, 'she will marry somebody with no heart and only one foot.'

'Excuse *me*, dear, I hadn't finished yet; if you could

kindly give me time to speak. The princess will lose her inheritance –'

'I *beg* your pardon; I was going to say that there will be a revolution –'

'*Will* you please be quiet, madam! There will *not* be a revolution – or at least, the princess herself will be lost long before that occurs – she will be poor and unknown and have to work for her living –'

'She'll marry one who has spent all his life in the open –'

'Oh, for gracious' sake! Didn't I just say she would marry somebody with only one foot?'

'The two things are not incompatible.'

'You don't very often find agricultural workers with only one foot.'

'Ladies, ladies!' said the king miserably, but not daring to be too abrupt with them, 'you have done enough harm to my poor child! Will you please continue your discussion somewhere else?'

The feuding fairies took their leave (so exhausted by their exhilarating quarrel that they both went home, retired to bed, and died next day) while, left alone, the poor king hung with tears in his eyes over his beautiful pink baby wondering what, if anything, could be done to avert the various bits of evil fortune that were coming to her. All that seemed to lie in his power was strict censorship of her presents, so as to make sure that she was never given a pig.

This he managed successfully until she was five years old, when her cousin came to stay with her. Lord Edwin Fitzlion was a spoilt, self-willed boy of about the same age as the princess; he was the seventh son of a seventh son; his brothers were all much older and had gone off into the world, his father had taken to big-game hunting and hardly ever came home, while his mother, tired of looking after boys and attending to shirts, schools, boots, and bats, was away on a three-year cruise. Lord Edwin had been left in the care of servants.

He was very beautiful, with dark velvety eyes and black hair; much better looking than his fat pink cousin; he was inclined to tease her. One day he overheard two equerries discussing the prophecies about her, and he became consumed with curiosity to see whether she would really turn into a pig if she were given one.

There were considerable difficulties about bringing pigs into the palace, but finally Edwin managed to buy a small one from a heavily bribed farmer. He smuggled it in, wrapped in brown paper and labelled *Inflatable rubber dinghy with outboard pump attachment.* Finding the nursery empty he undid the pig and let it loose, then rushed in search of Henrietta.

'Henry! come quick, I've brought a present for you.'

'Oh, where?'

'In the nursery! Hurry up!'

With rare politeness he stood aside to let her go in first and heard her squeak for joy as she ran through the door,

'Oh, it's a dear little pig –'

Then there was silence, except for more squeaks, and when Lord Edwin looked through the door he saw two little pigs, absolutely identical, sniffing noses in the most friendly way.

Lord Edwin was sent home in disgrace to his father's castle, where he proceeded to run wild, as his parents were still away. (In fact they never returned.) He spent all his time in the woods, riding his eldest brother's horse, Bayard, and flying his next brother's falcon, Ger. One day when far from home he saw a large hare sitting upright on the other side of a pool. Quickly he unhooded the falcon and prepared to fly her.

The hare said,

'You'll be sorry if you do that.'

'Oh, who cares for you,' said Edwin rudely, and he loosed Ger. But the falcon, instead of towering up and dropping on the hare, flew slantwise across the pond into some thick trees and vanished from view. Edwin's eyes followed the bird in annoyance and perplexity. When he looked back he saw that a little old man with an unfriendly expression was standing on the spot where the hare had been.

'You are a spoilt, ill-mannered boy,' the old man said. 'I know all about you and what you did to your cousin. You can stay where you are, learning a bit of patience and consideration, until a Home Secretary comes to rescue you.'

Nobody had been particularly fond of Edwin, so nobody missed him or inquired after him.

The king, of course, was heartbroken when he learned what had happened to his daughter. Numerous tests were carried out on the two little pigs, in an attempt to discover which one was the princess. They were put in little beds with peas under the mattresses but both rummaged out the peas and ate them in the course of the night. Dishes of pearls and potato-peelings were placed in front of them, in the hope that the princess would prefer the pearls, but they both dived unhesitatingly for the potato-peelings. The most eminent pig-breeders of the kingdom were brought in to scrutinize them, but with no result; they were two handsome pink little pigs, and that was all that could be said of them.

'Well,' said the king at length, 'one of them is my daughter, and she must receive the education due to a princess. Some day I suppose she will be restored to her proper shape, as she is to marry a one-footed man, poor dear –'

'The fairy didn't actually say a *man* with one foot,'
pointed out the Lord Chamberlain.

'Use your sense, man. What else could it be? Anyway
she must have a proper education. It would never do if
when she reverted to human shape she knew no more than
a child of five.'

So the little pigs sat seriously side by side on two little
chairs in the schoolroom and were taught and lectured at
by a series of learned professors and eminent school-
mistresses. No one could tell if any of this teaching sank
in, for they merely sat and gazed. If asked questions, they
grunted.

One day when the pigs were nearly fifteen, the king
came into the schoolroom.

'Hullo, my dears,' he said, 'how are you this morning?'
He patted his daughter and her friend, then sat down
wearily in an armchair to rest while they had their lunch.
Affairs of state were becoming very burdensome to him
these days.

A footman brought in two big blue bowls of pig-mash,
one in each hand. The pigs began to give piercing squeals
and rush about frantically, bumping into tables and chairs
and each other. Their attendant firmly collared them one
at a time, tied a white napkin round the neck of each, and
strapped them into two chairs. The bowls were put in
front of them and instantly there was such a guzzling and
a slupping and a splashing and a slobbering that nobody
could hear a word for five minutes until the bowls were
empty. Then the little pigs looked up again, beaming
with satisfaction, their faces covered in mash.

The footman solemnly stepped forward again and wiped
their faces clean with a cloth-of-gold flannel. Then they
were let out to play, and could be seen through the window whisking about the palace garden with tails tightly
curled, and chasing one another across the flower-beds.

The king sighed.

'It's no use,' he said, 'one must face facts. My daughter Henrietta is *not* an ordinary princess. And her friend Hermione is a very ordinary little pig. I am afraid that no prince, even a one-footed one, would ask for Henrietta's hand in marriage after seeing her eat her lunch. We must send them to a finishing school. They have had plenty of intellectual education – at least I suppose they have – it's time they acquired a little polish.'

So the two pigs were packed off (in hampers) to Miss Dorothea ffoulkes' Select Finishing School for the Daughters of the Aristocracy and Nobility.

At first all went well. The king received monthly re-reports which informed him that his daughter (and her friend) had learned to walk downstairs with books on their heads, to enter and leave rooms, get in and out of motor cars with grace and dignity, play the piano and the harp, waltz, cha-cha-cha, embroider, and ride side-saddle.

'Well, I've always heard that Miss ffoulkes was a marvel,' said the king, shaking his head with astonishment, 'but I never thought anyone could teach a pig to ride side-saddle. I can't wait to see them.'

But he had to wait, for Miss ffoulkes strictly forbade the parents of her pupils to visit them while they were being put through her course of training. The reason for this was that she had to treat the girls with such frightful severity, in order to drill the necessary elegance and deportment into them, that if they had been given the chance they would have implored their parents to take them away. Letters, however, were always written to the dictation of Miss ffoulkes herself, so there was no opportunity of complaining, and at the end of her course the debutantes were so grateful for their beautiful poise that all was forgotten and forgiven.

Miss ffoulkes nearly met her Waterloo in Henrietta and Hermione though. She managed to teach them tennis, bridge, and how to dispose of a canapé stick, but she could not teach them flower-arrangement. The pigs had no taste for it; they always ate the flowers.

One day they had been spanked and sent into the garden in disgrace after it was discovered that they had eaten a large bundle of lilies and asparagus-fern which they were supposed to build into a decorative creation. Sore and miserable they wandered down Miss ffoulkes's dreary gravel paths. Simultaneously they were seized by the same impulse. They wriggled through the hedge at the bottom of the garden and were seen no more at the Select School.

Instead of a final report on deportment the king had a note from Miss ffoulkes which said,

'I regret to announce that your daughter and her friend have committed the unpardonable social blunder of running away from my establishment. The police have been informed and will no doubt recover them for you in due course. Since this behaviour shows that our tuition has been thrown away on them your fees are returned herewith. (Cheque for £20,000 enc.) Your very obdt. srvt. Dorothea ffoulkes.'

In spite of all efforts, the police failed to trace the two little pigs. Advertisements in newspapers, on television and radio, pictures outside police stations, offers of rewards, brought no replies. The king was in terror, imagining his daughter and her friend innocently strolling into a bacon factory. He gave up all pretence at governing and spent his time in a desperate round of all the farms in the kingdom, gazing mournfully at pig after pig in the hope of recognizing Henrietta and Hermione. But none of the pigs responded to his greetings.

As a matter of fact Henrietta and her friend had gone

no farther than the garden of the house next door to Miss ffoulkes. There they had been rootling peacefully (but elegantly because their training had not been wasted) among the roses near the front gate when a young man in a white coat came out of the house, irritably listening to the parting words of a beautiful young lady with flowing dark hair.

'And don't forget,' she was saying earnestly, 'all your last experimental results are in the stack under the five-gramme weight, and the milk for tea is in the test-tube at the left-hand end of the right-hand rack, and the baby amoeba wants feeding again at five. Now I really must fly, for my fiancé becomes very annoyed if he is kept waiting.'

'Good-bye, Miss Snooks,' said the white-coated young man crossly, and he slammed the gate behind her. 'Why in the name of goodness do all my assistants have to get married? Not one of them has stayed longer than three months in the last three years.'

Then his eye fell on the two pigs, who were gazing at him attentively.

'Pigs,' he mused. 'I wonder if pigs could be taught to do the work? Pigs might not be so prone to become engaged. Pigs, would you consider a job as research assistants?'

The pigs liked his face; they followed him into the house, where he instructed them in the research work he was doing on cosmic rays.

'I shall have to teach you to talk, though,' he observed, 'for I can't put up with assistants who grunt all the time.'

He laid aside all his other work and devoted himself to teaching them; at the end of a week he had succeeded, for he was the most brilliant scientist and philosopher in the kingdom. In any case, nobody had ever considered teaching the pigs to talk before.

When they could speak the professor asked their names.

'One of us is Henrietta and one is Hermione, but we are not sure which is which,' they told him, 'for we were muddled up when we were young.'

'In that case I shall call you Miss X and Miss Y. Miss X, you will look after making the tea, feeding the amoeba, and filing the slides. Miss Y, you will turn away all visitors, keep the cosmic ray tuned, and polish the microscope. Both of you will make notes on my experiments.'

The two pigs now found their education of great value. They could carry piles of books and microscope slides about on their heads, curtsy gracefully to callers as they showed them the door, write notes in a neat little round hand, and play the piano and the harp to soothe the professor if his experiments were not going well. They were all very happy together, and the professor said that he had never before had such useful and talented assistants.

One day after about five years had passed in this manner, the professor raised his eye from the microscope, rubbed his forehead, looked at Miss Y, industriously taking notes, and Miss X, busily putting away slides, and said,

'Pigs, it occurs to me to wonder if you are really human beings turned into your present handy if humble form?'

'One of us is,' replied Miss Y, tucking her pencil behind her ear, 'but we don't know which.'

'It should be easy to change you back,' the professor remarked. 'I wonder I never thought of it before. We can just switch on the cosmic ray and rearrange your molecules.'

'Which of us?'

'You can both try, and I daresay nothing will happen to one of you.'

'Should we like that?' said the pigs to each other. 'You see we're used to being together,' they told the professor.

'Oh, come, come,' he exclaimed impatiently. 'If one of you is really human, it's her plain duty to change back, and the other one should not stand in her way.'

Thus admonished, both pigs walked in front of the ray, and both immediately turned into young ladies with pink faces, turned-up noses, fair hair, and intelligent blue eyes.

'Humph,' remarked the professor, 'that ray must be more powerful than I had allowed for; we do not seem to have advanced matters much farther.'

As the young ladies still did not know which of them was which, they continued to be called Miss X and Miss Y, and as they were very happy in their work they continued to help the professor.

One day Miss Y noticed a number of callers approaching the front door. Though she curtsied politely and did her best to turn them away, they insisted on entering the laboratory.

'Professor,' said a spokesman, 'we are the leaders of the Revolution, and we have come to invite you to be the first president of our new republic, since you are undoubtedly the wisest man in the country.'

'Oh good gracious,' said the professor, very much taken aback and frowning because he hated interruptions to his work, 'whatever possessed you to revolt, and what have you done with the king?'

'We revolted because it is the fashionable thing to do – all the other countries have done it ages ago – and the king retired last week; he has taken to farming. But now please step into the carriage which is waiting outside and we will escort you to the president's residence.'

'If I accept,' said the professor, 'it is understood that I must have unlimited time to pursue my research.'

'Yes, yes, you will need to do very little governing; just keep an eye on things and see that justice and reason prevail. Of course you can appoint anybody you choose to whatever government positions you wish.'

'In that case I shall appoint my two assistants, Miss X and Miss Y, to be the Home and Foreign Secretaries. I am certain that no one could be more competent.'

The new president's residence turned out to be none other than the castle of the Baron Fitzlion, long since deserted. Here the republican government was set up, and as none of the old officials had been removed from their posts, everything proceeded very smoothly, and the professor and his two assistants found ample time to continue their research on cosmic rays.

They were now investigating the use of the professor's ray projector on plant life; one day Miss X took a small portable projector into the woods nearby, proposing to make notes about differences in the ray's effect on coniferous and deciduous trees.

While scribbling in her notebook she heard a sneeze, and looked up to discover that a larch in front of her had developed a head. Two handsome black eyes gazed at her mournfully.

'Are you the Home Secretary?' the head inquired.

'Why, yes,' replied Miss X, controlling her natural surprise at such a question being put to her by a tree.

'In that case would you be so extremely kind as to liberate the rest of me with your camera, or whatever it is?'

'I'm afraid this portable projector isn't strong enough for that – it only runs off a battery. We shall have to build a larger one beside you and connect it to the mains; that will take two or three weeks.'

He sighed. 'Oh well, I've been here fifteen years, I daresay I can wait another three weeks. No doubt I deserved this fate for turning my poor little cousin into a pig, but I *am* so stiff.'

'Did you turn your cousin into a pig?' said Miss X with interest. 'I suppose that might have been me.'

'Were you turned into a pig?'

'Somebody was; we cannot be sure if it was my friend Miss Y or myself. You see, we are not certain which of us is which.'

'Henrietta was to lose her inheritance and go through a revolution.'

'So she has.'

'And be poor and unknown and earn her living.'

'We both are and do.'

'And marry a man with one foot. I'll tell you what,' said Lord Edwin, who had rapidly developed a tremendous admiration for Miss X's cheerful pink face and yellow hair – such a refreshing contrast to the leaves and branches which were all he had had to look at for the last fifteen years – 'I've only got one foot just now, you're standing on it; so if you marry me it will prove that you are the princess.'

'That's true,' she said thoughtfully, 'and then I shall be able to go and see poor Papa and tell him that I am me; there didn't seem much point in disturbing him until I had some more data.'

So the marriage ceremony between Lord Edwin and Miss X was performed while they were building the full-size cosmic ray projector nearby, and as soon as the bridegroom had been released they went to see the king, who was very contented on his farm and had no wish at all to resume governing.

'I have acquired a fondness for pigs after looking at so many,' he said. 'I am sure you young people can manage very well without me.'

So Lord Edwin became Prime Minister (having learned

thoughtfulness and civilized behaviour during his long spell in the woods). Miss Y, who was now known to be Hermione, married the professor, and they all governed happily ever after.

The Dark Streets of Kimball's Green

'EM! You, Em! Where has that dratted child got to? Em! Wait till I lay hold of you, I won't half tan you!'

Mrs Bella Vaughan looked furiously up and down the short street. She was a stocky woman, with short, thick, straight grey hair, parted on one side and clamped back by a grip; a cigarette always dangled from one corner of her mouth and, as soon as it dwindled down, another grew there. 'Em! Where have you got to?' she yelled again.

'Here I am, Mrs Vaughan!' Emmeline dashed anxiously round the corner.

'Took long enough about it! The Welfare Lady's here, wants to know how you're getting on. Here, let's tidy you up.'

Mrs Vaughan pulled a comb and handkerchief out of her tight-stretched apron pocket, dragged the comb sharply through Emmeline's hair, damped the handkerchief with spit and scrubbed it over Emmeline's flinching face.

'Hullo, Emmeline. Been out playing?' said the Welfare Lady, indoors. 'That's right. Fresh air's the best thing for them, isn't it, Mrs Vaughan?'

'She's always out,' grunted Mrs Vaughan. 'Morning, noon and night. I don't hold with kids frowsting about indoors. Not much traffic round here.'

'Well, Emmeline, how are you getting on? Settling down with Mrs Vaughan, quite happy, are you?'

Emmeline looked at her feet and muttered something. She was thin and small for her age, dark-haired and pale-cheeked.

'She's a mopey kid,' Mrs Vaughan pronounced. 'Always want to be reading, if I didn't tell her to run out of doors.'

'Fond of reading, are you?' the Welfare Lady said kindly. 'And what do you read, then?'

'Books,' muttered Emmeline. The Welfare Lady's glance strayed to the huge, untidy pile of magazines on the telly.

'Kid'll read anything she could lay hands on, if I let her,' Mrs Vaughan said. 'I don't though. What good does reading do you? None that I know of.'

'Well, I'm glad you're getting on all right, Emmeline. Be a good girl and do what Mrs Vaughan tells you. And I'll see you next month again.' She got into her tiny car and drove off to the next of her endless list of calls.

'Right,' said Mrs Vaughan. 'I'm off too, down to the town hall to play bingo. So you hop it, and mind you're here on the doorstep at eleven sharp or I'll skin you.'

Emmeline murmured something.

'Stay indoors? Not on your nelly! And have them saying, if the house burnt down, that I oughtn't to have left you on your own?'

'It's so cold out.' A chilly September wind scuffled the bits of paper in the street. Emmeline shivered in her thin coat.

'Well, run about then, and keep warm! Fresh air's good for you, like that interfering old busybody said. Anyway she's come and gone for the month, that's something. Go on, hop it now.'

So Emmeline hopped it.

Kimball's Green, where Mrs Vaughan had her home, was a curious, desolate little corner of London. It lay round the top of a hill, which was crowned with a crumbling, blackened church, St Chad's. The four or five streets of tiny, aged houses were also crumbling and blackened, all due for demolition, and most of them empty. The houses were so old that they seemed shrunk and wrinkled, like old apples or old faces, and they were immeasurably, unbelievably dirty, with the dirt of hundreds of years. Around the little hill was a flat, desolate tract of land, Wansea Marshes, which nobody had even tried to use until the nineteenth century; then it became covered with railway goods yards and brick-works and gas-works and an electric power station, all of which belched their black smoke over the little island of Kimball's Green on the hilltop.

You could hardly think anybody would *choose* to live in such a cut-off part; but Mrs Vaughan had been born in Sylvan Street, near the top of the hill, and she declared she wasn't going to shift until they came after her with a bulldozer. She took in foster children when they grew too old for the Wansea Orphanage, and, though it wasn't a very healthy neighbourhood, what with the smoke and the damp from the marshes, there were so many orphans, and so few homes for them to go to, that Emmeline was the latest of a large number who had stayed with Mrs Vaughan. But there were very few other children in the district now; very few inhabitants at all, except old and queer ones who camped secretly in the condemned houses. Most people found it too far to go to the shops: an eight-penny bus-ride, all the way past the goods yards and the gas-works, to Wansea High Street.

So far as anyone knew, Emmeline belonged in the neighbourhood; she had been found on the step of St Chad's one windy March night; but in spite of this, or because of it, she was rather frightened by the nest of little dark empty streets. She was frightened by many things, among which were Mrs Vaughan and her son Colin. And she particularly hated the nights, five out of seven, when Mrs Vaughan went off to play bingo, leaving

Emmeline outside in the street. Indeed, if it hadn't been for two friends, Emmeline really didn't know how she could have borne those evenings.

As Mrs Vaughan's clumping steps died away down the hill, one of the friends appeared: his thin form twined out from between some old black railings and he rubbed encouragingly against Emmeline's ankles, sticking up his tail in welcome.

'Oh, Scrawny! There you are,' she said with relief. 'Here, I've saved you a piece of cheese-rind from tea.'

Old Scrawny was a tattered, battered tabby, with ragged whiskers, crumpled ears, and much fur missing from his tail; he had no owner and lived on what he could find; he ate the cheese-rind with a lot of loud, vulgar, guzzling noise, and hardly washed at all afterwards; but Emmeline loved him dearly, and he loved her back. Every night she left her window open and old Scrawny climbed in, by various gutters, drain-pipes, and the wash-house roof. Mrs Vaughan wouldn't have allowed such a thing for a minute if she had known, but Emmeline always took care that old Scrawny had left long before she was called in the morning.

When the rind was finished Scrawny jumped into Emmeline's arms and she tucked her hands for warmth under his scanty fur; they went up to the end of the street by the church, where there was a telephone booth. Like the houses around it was old and dirty, and it had been out of order for so many years that now nobody even bothered to thump its box for coins. The only person who used it was Emmeline, and she used it almost every night, unless gangs were roaming the streets and throwing stones, in which case she hid behind a dustbin or under a flight of area steps. But when the gangs had gone else-where the call-box made a very convenient shelter; best of all, it was even light enough to read there, because although the bulb in the call-box had been broken long ago, a street lamp shone right overhead.

'No book tonight, Scrawny, unless Mr Yakkymo comes and brings me another,' said Emmeline, 'so what shall we do? Shall we phone somebody, or shall I tell you a story?'

Scrawny purred, dangling round her neck like a striped scarf.

'We'll ring somebody up, shall we? All right.'

She let the heavy door close behind her. Inside it was not exactly warm, but at least they were out of the wind. Scrawny climbed from Emmeline's shoulder into the compartment where the telephone books would have been if somebody hadn't made off with them; Emmeline picked up the broken receiver and dialled.

'Hullo, can I speak to King Cunobel? Hullo, King Cunobel, I am calling to warn you. A great army is approaching your fort – the Tribe of the Children of Darkness. Under their wicked queen Belavaun they are coming to attack your stronghold with spears and chariots. You must tell your men to be extra brave; each man must arm himself with his bow and a sheaf of arrows, two spears and a sword. Each man must have his faithful wolfhound by his side.' She stroked old Scrawny, who seemed to be listening intently. 'Your men are far out-numbered by the Children of Dark, King Cunobel, so you must tell your Chief Druid to prepare a magic drink, made from vetch and mallow and succory, to give them courage. The leaves must be steeped in mead and left to gather dew for two nights, until you have enough to wet each man's tongue. Then they will be brave enough to beat off the Children of Dark and save your camp.'

She listened for a moment or two with her ear pressed against the silent receiver, and then said to old Scrawny,

'King Cunobel wants to know what will happen if the

Children of Dark get to the fort before the magic drink is prepared?'

'Morow,' said Scrawny. He jumped down from the bookshelf and settled himself on Emmeline's feet, where there was more room to stretch out.

'My faithful wolfhound says you must order your men to make high barricades of brambles and thorns,' Emmeline told King Cunobel. 'Build them in three rings round the encampment, and place one-third of your men inside each ring. King Cunobel and the Druids will be in the middle ring. Each party must fight to the death in order to delay the Children of Dark until the magic drink is ready. Do you understand? Then good-bye and good luck.'

She listened again.

'He wants to know who *I* am,' she told Scrawny, and she said into the telephone, 'I am a friend, the Lady Emmeline, advised by her faithful enchanted wolfhound Catuscraun. I wish you well.'

Then she rang off and said to Scrawny, 'Do you think I had better call the Chief Druid and tell him to hurry up with that magic drink?'

Old Scrawny shut his eyes.

'No,' she agreed, 'you're right, it would only distract him. I know, I'll ring up the wicked Queen of Dark.'

She dialed again and said.

'Hullo, is that the wicked Queen Belavaun? This is your greatest enemy, ringing up to tell you that you will never, never capture the stronghold of King Cunobel. Not if you besiege it for three thousand years! King Cunobel has a strong magic that will defeat you. All your tribes, the Trinovans and the Votadins and the Damnons and the Bingonii will be eaten by wolves and wild boars. Not a man will remain! And you will lose all your wealth and power and your purple robes and fur cloaks, you will have nothing left but a miserable old mud cabin outside King Cunobel's stronghold, and every day his men will look over the walls and laugh at you. Goodbye, and bad luck to you forever!'

She rang off and said to Scrawny, 'That frightened her.'

Scrawny was nine-tenths asleep, but at this moment footsteps coming along the street made him open his eyes warily. Emmeline was alert, too. The call-box made a good look-out point, but it would be a dangerous place in which to be trapped.

'It's all right,' she said to Scrawny, then. 'It's only Mr Yakkymo.'

She opened the door and they went to meet their other friend.

Mr Yakkymo (he spelt his name Iachimo, but Yakkymo was the way it sounded) came limping slightly up the street until he reached them; then he rubbed the head of old Scrawny (who stuck his tail up) and handed Emmeline a book. It was old and small, with a mottled binding and gilt-edged leaves; it was called *The Ancient History of Kimball's Green and Wansea Marshes*, and it came from Wansea Borough Library.

Emmeline's eyes opened wide with delight. She began reading the book at once, skipping from page to page.

'Why, this tells all about King Cunobel! It's even better than the one you brought about ancient London. Have you read this, Mr Yakkymo?'

He nodded, smiling. He was a thin, bent old man with rather long white hair; as well as the book he carried a leather case, which contained a flute, and when he was not speaking he would often open this case and run his fingers absently up and down the instrument.

'I thought you would find it of interest,' he said. 'It's a pity Mrs Vaughan won't let you go to the public library yourself.'

'She says reading only puts useless stuck-up notions in people's heads,' Emmeline said dreamily, her eyes darting up and down the pages of the book. 'Listen! It tells what King Cunobel wore – a short kilt with a gold belt. His chest was painted blue with woad, and he had a gold collar round his neck and a white cloak with gold embroidery. He carried a shield of beaten brass and a short sword. On his head he wore a fillet of gold, and on his arm gold armlets. His house was built of mud and stone, with a thatched roof; the walls were hung with skins and the floor strewn with rushes.'

They had turned and were walking slowly along the street; old Scrawny, after the manner of cats, sometimes loitered behind investigating doorsteps and dark crannies, sometimes darted ahead and then waited for them to come up with him.

'Do you think any of King Cunobel's descendants still live here?' Emmeline said.

'It is just possible.'

'Tell me some more about what it was like here then.'

'All the marshes – the part where the brick-works and the goods yards are now – would have been covered by forest and threaded by slow-flowing streams.'

'Threaded by slow-flowing streams,' Emmeline murmured to herself.

'All this part would be Cunobel's village. Little mud huts, each with a door and a chimney hole, thatched with reeds.'

Emmeline looked at the pavements and rows of houses, trying to imagine them away, trying to imagine forest trees and little thatched huts.

'There would be a stockade of logs and thorns all round. A bigger hall for the king, and one for the Druids near the sacred grove.'

'Where was that?'

'Up at the top of the hill, probably. With a specially sacred oak in the middle. There is an oak tree, still, in St Chad's churchyard; maybe it's sprung from an acorn of the Druids' oak.'

'Maybe it's the same one? Oaks live a long time, don't they?'

'Hark!' he said checking. 'What's that?'

The three of them were by the churchyard wall; they kept still and listened. Next moment they all acted independently, with the speed of long practice: Mr Iachimo, murmuring, 'Good night, my child,' slipped away round a corner; Emmeline wrapped her precious book in a polythene bag and poked it into a hole in the wall behind a loose stone; then she and old Scrawny raced downhill, back to Mrs Vaughan's house. She crouched panting on the doorstep, old Scrawny leapt up on to a shed roof and out of reach, just as a group of half a dozen people came swaggering and singing along the street.

'What was that?' one of them called.

'A cat.'

'Let's go after it!'

'No good. It's gone.'

When they got to Mrs Vaughan's their chief left the others and came over to Emmeline.

'It's you, is it, Misery?' he said. 'Where's Ma?'

'Out at bingo.'

'She would be. I wanted to get a bit of the old girl's pension off her before she spent it all.'

He gave Emmeline's hair a yank and flipped her nose, hard and painfully, with his thumbnail. She looked at him in stony silence, biting her lip.

'Who's *she*, Col?' a new gang-member asked. 'Shall we chivvy her?'

'She's one of my Ma's orphanage brats – just a little drip.

Ma won't let me tease her, so long as she's indoors, or on the step. But watch it, you, if we catch you in the street.' Colin flipped Emmeline's nose again and they drifted off, kicking at anything that lay on the pavement.

At half-past eleven Mrs Vaughan came home from her bingo and let in the shivering Emmeline, who went silently up to her bed in the attic. At eleven thirty-five old Scrawny jumped with equal silence on to her stomach, and the two friends curled round each other for warmth.

*

Colin was not at breakfast next morning. Often he spent nights on end away from home; his mother never bothered to ask where.

Emmeline had to run errands and do housework in the morning but in the afternoon Mrs Vaughan, who wanted a nap, told her to clear off and not show her face a minute before six. That gave her five whole hours for reading; she dragged on her old coat and flew up to the church-yard.

The door in the high black wall was always kept locked, but somebody had once left a lot of rusty old metal pipes stacked in an angle of the wall; Emmeline, who weighed very little more than old Scrawny, clambered carefully up them, and so over.

Inside, the churchyard was completely overgrown. Blackthorn, plane and sycamore trees were entangled with great clumps of bramble. Groves of mares'-tails, chin-high to Emmeline, covered every foot of the ground. It made a perfect place to come and hide by day, but was too dark at night and too full of pitfalls; pillars and stone slabs leaned every which way, hidden in the vegetation.

Emmeline flung herself down on the flat tomb of Admiral Sir Horace Tullesley Campbell and read her book; for three hours she never moved; then she closed it with a sigh, so as to leave some for the evening in case Mrs Vaughan went out.

A woodpecker burst yammering from the tallest tree as Emmeline shut the book. Could that be the Druids' oak, she wondered, and started to push her way through to it. Brambles scratched her face and tore her clothes; Mrs Vaughan would punish her but that couldn't be helped. And at last she was there. The tree stood in a little clear space of bare leaf-mould. It was an oak, a big one, with a gnarled, massive trunk and roots like knuckles thrusting out of the ground. This made an even better secret place for reading than the Admiral's tomb, and Emmeline wished once again that it wasn't too dark to read in the churchyard at night.

St Chad's big clock said a quarter to six, so she left *The Ancient History of Kimball's Green* in its plastic bag hidden in a hollow of the tree and went draggingly home; then realized, too late, that her book would be exceedingly hard to find once dark had fallen.

Mrs Vaughan, who had not yet spent all her week's money, went out to bingo again that evening, so Emmeline returned to the telephone box and rang up King Cunobel.

'Is that the King? I have to tell you that your enemies are five miles nearer. Queen Belavaun is driving a chariot with scythes on its wheels, and her wicked son Coluon leads a band of savage followers; he carries a sling and a gold-handled javelin and is more cruel than any of the band. Has the Chief Druid prepared the magic drink yet?'

She listened and old Scrawny, who as usual was sitting at her feet, said 'Prtnrow?'

'The Chief Druid says they have made the drink, Scrawny, and put it in a flagon of beaten bronze, which has been set beneath the sacred oak until it is needed. Meanwhile the warriors are feasting on wheat-cakes, boars' flesh and mead.'

Next she rang up Queen Belavaun and hissed, 'Oh wicked queen, your enemies are massing against you! You think that you will triumph, but you are wrong! Your son will be taken prisoner, and you will be turned out of your kingdom; you will be forced to take refuge with the Iceni or the Brigantes.'

It was still only half-past nine, and Mr Iachimo probably would not come this evening, for two nights out of three he went to play his flute outside a theatre in the West End of London.

'Long ago I was a famous player and people came from all over Europe to hear me,' he had told Emmeline sadly, one wet evening when they were sheltering together in the church porch.

'What happened? Why aren't you famous now?'

'I took to drink,' he said mournfully. 'Drink gives you hiccups. You can't play the flute with hiccups.'

'You don't seem to have hiccups now.'

'Now I can't afford to drink any longer.'

'So you can play the flute again,' Emmeline said triumphantly.

'True,' he agreed; he pulled out his instrument and blew a sudden dazzling shower of notes into the rainy dark. 'But now it is too late. Nobody listens; nobody remembers the name of Iachimo. And I have grown too old and tired to make them remember.'

'Poor Mr Yakkymo,' Emmeline thought, recalling this conversation. '*He* could do with a drop of King Cunobel's magic drink; then he'd be able to make people listen to him.'

She craned out of the telephone box to look at St Chad's clock: quarter to ten. The streets were quiet tonight; Colin's gang had got money from somewhere and were down at the Wansea Palais.

'I'm going to get my book,' Emmeline suddenly decided. 'At least I'm going to try. There's a moon, it shouldn't be too dark to see. Coming, Scrawny?'

Scrawny intimated, stretching, that he didn't mind.

The churchyard was even stranger under the moon than by daylight; the mares'-tails threw their zebra-striped shadows everywhere and an owl flew hooting across the path; old Scrawny yakkered after it indignantly to come back and fight fair, but the owl didn't take up his challenge.

'I don't suppose it's really an owl,' Emmeline whispered. 'Probably one of Queen Belavaun's spies. We must make haste.'

Finding the oak tree was not so hard as she had feared, but finding the book was a good deal harder, because under the tree's thick leaves and massive branches no light could penetrate; Emmeline groped and fumbled among the roots until she was quite sure she must have been right round the tree at least three times. At last her right hand slipped into a deep crack; she rummaged about hopefully, her fingers closed on something, but what she pulled out was a small round object, tapered at one end. She stuck it in her coat pocket and went on searching. 'The book must be here somewhere, Scrawny; unless Queen Belavaun's spy has stolen it.'

At last she found it; tucked away where she could have sworn she had searched a dozen times already.

'Thank goodness! Now we'd better hurry, or there won't be any time for reading after all.'

Emmeline was not sorry to leave the churchyard behind; it felt *crowded*, as if King Cunobel's warriors were hiding there, shoulder to shoulder among the bushes, keeping vigilant watch; Sylvan Street outside was empty and lonely in comparison. She scurried into the phone box, clutching Scrawny against her chest.

'Now listen while I read to you about the Druids, Scrawny: they wore long white robes and they liked mistletoe – there's some mistletoe growing on that oak tree, I'm positive! – and they used rings of sacred stones, too. Maybe some of the stones in the churchyard are left over from the Druids.'

Scrawny purred agreeingly, and Emmeline looked up the hill, trying to move St Chad's church out of the way and replace it by a grove of sacred trees with aged, white-robed men among them.

Soon it was eleven o'clock: time to hide the book behind the stone and wait for Mrs Vaughan on the door-step. Along with his mother came Colin, slouching and bad tempered.

'Your face is all scratched,' he told Emmeline. 'You look a sight.'

'What have you been up to?' Mrs Vaughan said sharply.

Emmeline was silent but Colin said, 'Reckon it's that mangy old cat she's always lugging about.'

'Don't let me see you with a cat round *this* house,' Mrs Vaughan snapped. 'Dirty, sneaking things, never know where they've been. If any cat comes in here, I tell you, I'll get Colin to wring its neck!'

Colin smiled; Emmeline's heart turned right over with horror. But she said nothing and crept off upstairs to bed; only, when Scrawny arrived later, rather wet because it had begun to rain, she clutched him convulsively tight; a few tears wouldn't make much difference to the dampness of his fur.

*

'Humph!' said Mrs Vaughan, arriving early and un-expectedly in Emmeline's attic. 'I thought as much!'

She leaned to slam the window but Scrawny, though startled out of sleep, could still move ten times faster than any human; he was out and over the roof in a flash.

'Look at that!' said Mrs Vaughan. 'Filthy, muddy cat's footprints all over my blankets! Well that's one job you'll do this morning, my young madam – you'll wash those blankets. And you'll have to sleep without blankets till they've dried – I'm not giving you any other. Daresay they're all full of fleas' eggs too.'

Emmeline, breakfastless, crouched over the tub in the back wash-house; she did not much mind the job, but her brain was giddy with worry about Scrawny; how could she protect him? Suppose he were to wait for her, as he sometimes did, outside the house. Mrs Vaughan had declared that she would go after him with the chopper if she set eyes on him; Colin had sworn to hunt him down.

'All right, hop it now,' Mrs Vaughan said, when the blankets satisfied her. 'Clear out, don't let me see you again before six. No dinner? Well, I can't help that, can I? You should have finished the washing by dinner-time. Oh, all right, here's a bit of bread and marge, now make yourself scarce. I can't abide kids about the house all day.'

Emmeline spent most of the afternoon in a vain hunt for Scrawny. Perhaps he had retired to some hidey-hole for a nap, as he often did at that time of day; but perhaps Colin had caught him already?

'Scrawny, Scrawny,' she called softly and despairingly at the mouths of alleys, outside gates, under trees and walls; there was no reply. She went up to the churchyard, but a needle in a hundred haystacks would be easier to find than Scrawny in that wilderness if he did not choose to wake and show himself.

Giving up for the moment Emmeline went in search of

Mr Iachimo, but he was not to be found either; he had never told Emmeline where he lived and was seldom seen by daylight; she thought he probably inhabited one of the condemned houses and was ashamed of it.

It was very cold; a grey, windy afternoon turning gloomily to dusk. Emmeline pushed cold hands deep in her pockets; her fingers met and explored a round, unusual object. Then she remembered the thing she had picked up in the dark under the oak tree. She pulled it out, and found she was holding a tiny flask, made of some dark lustreless metal tarnished with age and crusted with earth. It was not quite empty; when Emmeline shook it she could hear liquid splashing about inside, but very little, not more than a few drops.

'Why,' she breathed, just for a moment forgetting her fear in the excitement of this discovery, 'it is – it *must* be the Druids' magic drink! But why, why didn't the warriors drink it?'

She tried to get out the stopper; it was made of some hard blackish substance, wood, or leather that had become hard as wood in the course of years.

'Can I help you, my child?' said a gentle voice above her head.

Emmeline nearly jumped out of her skin – but it was only Mr Iachimo, who had hobbled silently up the street.

'Look – look, Mr Yakkymo! Look what I found under the big oak in the churchyard! It must be the Druids' magic drink – mustn't it? Made of mallow and vetch and succory, steeped in mead, to give warriors courage. It must be!'

He smiled at her; his face was very kind. 'Yes, indeed it must!' he said.

But somehow, although he was agreeing with her, for a moment Emmeline had a twinge of queer dread, as if there were nothing – nothing at all – left in the world to hold on to; as if even Mr Iachimo were not what he seemed but, perhaps, a spy sent by Queen Belavaun to steal the magic flagon.

Then she pushed down her fear, taking a deep breath, and said, 'Can you get the stopper out, Mr Yakkymo?'

'I can try,' he said, and brought out a tiny foreign-looking penknife shaped like a fish with which he began prising at the fossil-hard black substance in the neck of the bottle. At last it began to crumble.

'Take care – do take care,' Emmeline said. 'There's only a very little left. Perhaps the defenders did drink most of it. But anyway there's enough left for you, Mr Yakkymo.'

'For me, my child? Why for me?'

'Because you need to be made brave so that you can make people listen to you play your flute.'

'Very true,' he said thoughtfully. 'But do not you need bravery too?'

Emmeline's face clouded. 'What good would bravery do me?' she said. '*I'm* all right – it's old Scrawny I'm worried about. Oh, Mr Yakkymo, Colin and Mrs Vaughan say they are going to *kill* Scrawny. What can I do?'

'You must tell them they have no right to.'

'*That* wouldn't do any good,' Emmeline said miserably. 'Oh! – You've got it out!'

The stopper had come out, but it had also crumbled away entirely.

'Never mind,' Emmeline said. 'You can put in a bit of the cotton-wool that you use to clean your flute. What does it smell of, Mr Yakkymo?'

His face had changed as he sniffed; he looked at her oddly. 'Honey and flowers,' he said.

Emmeline sniffed too. There was a faint – very faint – aromatic, sweet fragrance.

'Wet your finger, Mr Yakkymo, and lick it! Please do! It'll help you, I know it will!'

'Shall I?'

'Yes, do, do!'

He placed his finger across the opening, and quickly turned the bottle upside down and back, then looked at his fingertip. There was the faintest drop of moisture on it.

'Quick – don't waste it,' Emmeline said, breathless with anxiety.

He licked his finger.

'Well? Does it taste?'

'No taste.' But he smiled, and bringing out a wad of cotton tissue, stuffed a piece of it into the mouth of the flask, which he handed to Emmeline.

'This is yours, my child. Guard it well! Now, as to your friend Scrawny – I will go and see Mrs Vaughan tomorrow, if you can protect him until then.'

'Thank you!' she said. 'The drink *must* be making you brave!'

Above their heads the clock of St Chad had tolled six.

'I must be off to the West End,' Mr Iachimo said. 'And you had better run home to supper. Till tomorrow, then – and a thousand, thousand thanks for your help.'

He gave her a deep, foreign bow and limped, much faster than usual, away down the hill.

'Oh, do let it work,' Emmeline thought, looking after him.

Then she ran home to Mrs Vaughan's.

Supper was over; Colin, thank goodness, did not come in, and Mrs Vaughan wanted to get through and be off; Emmeline bolted down her food, washed the plates, and was dismissed to the streets again.

As she ran up to the churchyard wall, with her fingers tight clenched round the precious little flask, a worrying thought suddenly struck her.

The magic drink had mead in it. Suppose the mead were to give Mr Iachimo hiccups? But there must be very little mead in such a tiny drop, she consoled herself; the risk could not be great.

When she pulled her book from the hole in the wall a sound met her ears that made her smile with relief: old Scrawny's mew of greeting, rather creaking and scratchy, as he dragged himself yawning, one leg at a time, from a clump of ivy on top of the wall.

'*There* you are, Scrawny! If you knew how I'd been worrying about you!'

She tucked him under one arm, put the book under the other, and made her way to the telephone box. Scrawny settled on her feet for another nap, and she opened *The History of Kimball's Green*. Only one chapter remained to be read; she turned to it and became absorbed. St Chad's clock ticked solemnly round overhead.

When Emmeline finally closed the book, tears were running down her face.

'Oh, Scrawny – they didn't win! They *lost*! King Cunobel's men were all killed – and the Druids too, defending the stronghold. Every one of them. Oh, how can I bear it? Why did it have to happen, Scrawny?'

Scrawny made no answer, but he laid his chin over her ankle. At that moment the telephone bell rang.

Emmeline stared at the instrument in utter consternation. Scrawny sprang up; the fur along his back slowly raised, and his ears flattened. The bell went on ringing.

'But', whispered Emmeline, staring at the broken black receiver, 'it's out of order. It *can't* ring! It's never rung! What shall I do, Scrawny?'

By now, Scrawny had recovered. He sat himself down again and began to wash. Emmeline looked up and down the empty street. Nobody came. The bell went on ringing.

*

At that same time, down below the hill and some distance off, in Wansea High Street, ambulance attendants were carefully lifting an old man off the pavement and laying him on a stretcher.

'Young brutes,' said a bystander to a policeman who was taking notes. 'It was one of those gangs of young hooligans from up Kimball's Green way; I'd know several of them again if I saw them. They set on him – it's the old street musician who comes up from there too. Seems he was coming home early tonight, and the boys jumped on him – you wouldn't think they'd bother with a poor fellow like him, he can't have much worth stealing.'

But the ambulance men were gathering up handfuls of half-crowns and two-shilling pieces which had rolled from Mr Iachimo's pockets; there were notes as well, ten shillings, a pound, even five- and ten-pound notes. And a broken flute.

'It was certainly worth their while tonight,' the policeman said. 'He must have done a lot better than usual.'

'He was a game old boy – fought back like a lion; marked some of them, I shouldn't wonder. They had to leave him and run for it. Will he be all right?'

'We'll see,' said the ambulance man, closing the doors.

*

'I'd better answer it,' Emmeline said at last. She picked up the receiver, trembling as if it might give her a shock.

'Hullo?' she whispered.

And a voice – a faint, hoarse, distant voice – said,

'This is King Cunobel. I cannot speak for long. I am calling to warn you. There is danger on the way – great danger coming towards you and your friend. Take care! Watch well!'

Emmeline's lips parted. She could not speak.

'There is danger – danger!' the voice repeated. Then the line went silent.

Emmeline stared from the silent telephone to the cat at her feet.

'Did you hear it too, Scrawny?'

Scrawny gazed at her impassively, and washed behind his ear.

Then Emmeline heard the sound of running feet. The warning had been real. She pushed the book into her pocket and was about to pick up Scrawny, but hesitated, with her fingers on the little flask.

'Maybe I ought to drink it, Scrawny? Better that than have it fall into the enemy's hands. Should I? Yes, I will! Here, you must have a drop too.'

She laid a wet finger on Scrawny's nose; out came his pink tongue at once. Then she drained the bottle, picked up Scrawny, opened the door, and ran.

Turning back once more to look she could see a group of dark figures coming after her down the street. She heard someone shout,

'That's her, and she's got the cat too! Come on!'

But beyond, behind and *through* her pursuers, Emmeline caught a glimpse of something else: a high, snow-covered hill, higher than the hill she knew, crowned with great bare trees. And on either side of her, among and in front of the dark houses, as if she were seeing two pictures, one printed on top of the other, were still more trees, and little thatched stone houses. Thin animals with red eyes slunk silently among the huts. Just a glimpse she had, of the two worlds, one behind the other, and then she had reached Mrs Vaughan's doorstep and turned to face the attackers.

Colin Vaughan was in the lead; his face, bruised, cut, and furious, showed its ugly intention as plainly as a raised club.

'Give me that damn cat. I've had enough from you and your friends. I'm going to wring its neck.'

But Emmeline stood at bay; her eyes blazed defiance and so did Scrawny's; he bared his fangs at Colin like a sabre-toothed tiger.

Emmeline said clearly, 'Don't you dare lay a finger on me, Colin Vaughan. Just don't you dare touch me!'

He actually flinched, and stepped back half a pace; his gang shuffled back behind him.

At this moment Mrs Vaughan came up the hill; not at her usual smart pace but slowly, plodding, as if she had no heart in her.

'Clear out, the lot of you,' she said angrily. 'Poor old Mr Iachimo's in the Wansea Hospital, thanks to you. Beating up old men! That's all you're good for. Go along, scram, before I set the back of my hand to some of you. Beat it!'

'But we were going to wring the cat's neck. You wanted me to do that,' Colin protested.

'Oh, what do I care about the blame cat?' she snapped, turning to climb the steps, and came face to face with Emmeline.

'Well, don't *you* stand there like a lump,' Mrs Vaughan said angrily. 'Put the blasted animal down and get to bed!'

'I'm not going to bed,' Emmeline said. 'I'm not going to live with you any more.'

'Oh, indeed? And where are you going, then?' said Mrs Vaughan, completely astonished.

'I'm going to see poor Mr Yakkymo. And then I'm going to find someone who'll take me and Scrawny, some place where I shall be happy. I'm never coming back to your miserable house again.'

'Oh, well, suit yourself,' Mrs Vaughan grunted. 'You're not the only one. I've just heard: fifty years in this place and then fourteen days' notice to quit; in two weeks the bulldozers are coming.'

She went indoors.

But Emmeline had not listened; clutching Scrawny, brushing past the gang as if they did not exist, she ran for the last time down the dark streets of Kimball's Green.